Moon People
2

Moon People 2

2

Mars Reborn

Dale M. Courtney

Amazon rated Moon People with 5 Stars

To order additional copies of this book, contact:
Xlibris Corporation
1-888-795-4274
www.Xlibris.com
Orders@Xlibris.com
52314

I would like to dedicate this book to my children. Whom I will always love no matter what. You can do anything you want to in this life, all you have to do is have the will and make it happen.

INTRODUCTION

Moon People 2

THIS STORY IS about the space Adventures of 1st Science Officer Captain David Braymer and his transition from the Lunar Base 1 base station to his new home the Powleens traded them called the Aurora Moon ship also known as the "Goddess of Dawn", it resembles a Moon and is 10 kilometers in diameter and with light speed capability. It's the size of a small city. It has everything a small city would have like two hospitals and restaurants and shopping malls all over the ship. Commander Braymer also has a romantic attachment to a young lady by the name of Lieutenant Heather Courtney who is an Officers Aid. They have a few out of the ordinary experiences that they do not forget any time soon. And our new friends the Powleens have advanced us centuries ahead of our time. They also traded us for five of their newest ships in their space fleet all with light speed capability with all of their weapons in tacked. They traded us for all kinds of their gadgetry and even some of their food. That's what they do. They go all over the galaxy looking for friends and ultimate knowledge and trade with everyone they can find. Commander Braymer also has a mission to do a genesis on Mars that turns out surprisingly good with a few added benefits. One of the benefits was discovering a lot of Martian people and animals in a Noah Ark kind of setup that has been frozen for over 100,000 years in life support chambers who were all brought back to life again. There were many discoveries' not to mention all of the futuristic weapons they find with aircraft all superior to anything at present by anyone. Nobody expected the Martians to have special mental powers like telekinetic and telekinesis and all sorts of mental telepathy powers. Like mind transference and the power to levitate in the air. Well everything was going pretty smooth until galactic war breaks out all over the galaxy and the final battle happens in our solar system. It was Earth with the Powleen people and also the Martians against the snake looking people called the Arcons and their friends the Thracians who resemble dog like people with sharp claws. There were crashed ships all over our planets and their Moons in our solar system. It was the battle of all battles It decided the control of our galaxy.

If you think all of this sounds good, wait till you read the book, its action packed from start to finish. I know you will enjoy Moon People one and two. It's some of my best work. Don't worry some day you just might see something that resembles "Moon People 3" coming to your local theater near you. Thank you and God Bless.

D.M.Courtney
Author

Table of Contents

CHAPTER 1

Mars Reborn

THIS STORY BEGINS off the planet of Mars where the Lunar Base 1 has positioned itself for 6 mouths of exploration and study for a possible genesis for colonization. So far Mars Base has found that under the surface of Mars are large cavities of ice. Also Mars Base has found that the lava core has cooled off over the centuries. They also found that Mars magnetic field is very low and the rotation of the planet has slowed to an abnormal speed. First Science Officer Captain David Braymer and the crew of the Lunar Base 1 are about to implement an experiment that will heat up the core of Mars and raise its magnetic field. Also melt the ice cavity underneath the surface, that should create oxygen through out the planet if all goes well. Also by heating up the core in the right spot should increase the speed of rotation of the planet. This is one of the areas that we are a little worried about in the experiment.

The Mars Base will be monitoring everything down on Mars and we will be monitoring everything from space. We do not really know exactly how much we need to heat up the core. We have a few differences of opinions. We are going to use a microwave beam to heat up the core at three-second intervals. The beam itself has the strength of 200,000 watts once it leaves the ship. By the time it hits the surface the strength is about 50,000 watts and by the time it gets through to the core the power level is about 20,000 watts.

On the bridge of the Lunar Base 1, Admiral Benson is in command. (Admiral Benson) Let's put everything on the main viewer Lieutenant Parsons.

Lieutenant Fisher are we ready to implement the microwave beam yet? Lieutenant Fisher answered, we are just about ready sir. Captain Braymer have you aligned the beam to the co ordinance of 45N32'17" and 85W22'46"? Yes ma'am, Captain Braymer replied. Lieutenant Fisher we are go for microwave beam as soon as we go over a few small details. Then Admiral Benson asked, Captain Braymer when we begin how exactly do you wish me to proceed from here? Would you brief me one more time? What I mean by that is do you want me to gap the intervals every ten seconds or five or what? I know you have everything ready. Captain Braymer answered well sir, I would like to try it like this. We hit the core with the beam for three seconds and then I will monitor the cores temperature and oxygen levels and its magnetic field and also rotation speed and check with Mars Base and we will go from there if we need more of the beam or stop. Then Admiral Benson said, ok that sounds logical Captain, lets precede then. Ok Lieutenant Fisher are you ready on the beam? Yes sir Lieutenant Fisher answered.

Then Admiral Benson said, On my mark. Ok Lieutenant fire that beam for a three second interval. (Lieutenant Fisher) Yes sir, beam has been engaged sir. (Captain Braymer) Sir the core has increased its temperature 8 degrees. There is no change of the rotation speed and no oxygen either sir. Also no change in the magnetic field sir I recommend that we increase the time to 10 seconds sir. (Admiral Benson) Ok, is everyone ready? Captain Braymer and Lieutenant Fisher said we're all go here sir. (Admiral Benson) Affirmative, let's fire that beam for ten seconds Lieutenant. (Lieutenant Fisher) Firing the microwave beam now sir. Ten seconds went by an Captain Braymer said Admiral we now have a 30 degree increase in core temperature and we are showing a 3% increase in the magnetic field. We are also showing a minor increase in speed to one half kilometer per hour sir, and the planet is stable, Admiral. (Admiral Benson) Captain what do you think? (Captain Braymer) Well sir, the ideal speed would be about 25 more kilometers an hour on the rotation speed. Also sir, I show no increase in oxygen either. Admiral the fact that we see an increase in speed of one half kilometer in rotation and an increase in the magnetic field shows that its working and the planet looks stable. Mars Base verifies that we are stable. We also would like to increase the core temperature another 1500 to 3000 degrees sir. Admiral let's try three 10-second intervals and check our readings. (Admiral Benson) Affirmative Captain. Ok are you ready Lieutenant Fisher? (Lieutenant Fisher) Yes sir. (Admiral Benson) Ok go ahead Lieutenant. (Lieutenant Fisher) Implementing sir. First 10 seconds complete, second ten seconds complete, Final ten seconds is completed sir. (Admiral Benson) Captain how are we looking? (Captain Braymer) Sir we have an increase of core temperature of 8 hundred degrees, and our magnetic field has increase to 27%. Our rotation speed has increased 8 kilometers an hour. (Lieutenant Parsons) Sir, look at the surface of the planet it looks like it's starting to smoke sir. (Captain Braymer) No Lieutenant I believe that's ice melting and what you see is water evaporating and making oxygen or steam as soon as it hits the surface atmosphere. Of course there are other gases and debris mixed in. But it should settle rather quickly once the affects of the sun start hitting the steam. Sir the experiment is starting to work. I'm showing signs of oxygen levels on the surface of Mars too sir. And so is the Mars base. It's a small amount but its oxygen.

(Admiral Benson) Captain that's incredible. Congratulation Captain. Do we try for double or nothing? Well sir the planet shows its stable and everything looks good. The Mars base reports that everything is go. Yes I think we should sir. (Admiral Benson) Ok Captain, I will do this but I recommend after we do this lets study the planet for a few days on what we have done. I just don't want to press our luck. (Captain Braymer) Sounds good sir. (Admiral Benson) Ok are you ready Lieutenant Fisher? (Lieutenant Fisher) Yes sir. (Admiral Benson) Go ahead and do it one more time Lieutenant (Lieutenant Fisher) Yes Admiral. Implementing Sir. First ten seconds complete, second ten seconds complete, final ten seconds is completed sir. Everyone said look at Mars and all of a sudden the planet's surface was spewing steam into the atmosphere several places all over the surface and it was all steaming up the entire atmosphere where you couldn't see the surface of Mars any more.

(Admiral Benson) Well Captain what do you think, what are your instruments saying. Captain Braymer answered, Sir it looks worse than it is. We are looking good on everything sir. Mar's magnetic field strength has increased 47% our rotation speed has increased to 20 kilometers an hour from the entire test. Our core temperature has increased to 2000 degrees and steady. Sir, Mars now has enough oxygen and can now sustain human life, and our Mars base technicians acknowledge that too sir. The Mars base affirms that there are still high levels of alkalis and a lot of acidity, Sulfur Dioxide, Methane and some other gases in the air. They recommend waiting and studying for a few days too sir. Before we start testing it with real humans. Their also saying they can't see their hand right in front of their face, but their saying oxygen levels are way above normal sir. Our computers are saying the same thing and core temperature is steady and stable. It just all needs to settle and clear up sir. (Admiral Benson) Ok everyone let's stop where we are and call it a day. Lets study what we have going now and let everything settle. Let's have a little celebration tonight in the Red Star lounge after we all get a little bit to eat and some rest. How about 20:00? If that sounds ok then I guess congratulations are in order captain it appears that your experiment was a major success. and we might now have a new planet to colonize. That's unbelievable. This is one of the most historical events ever. It's right up there with meeting the Powleens and getting light speed technology. You know we really are going into the Age of Aquarius. Lieutenant Courtney contact Earth and tell them the good news. Tell them so far everything looks great. When the storms clear, and in about a week of studying Mars. We are going to launch a shuttle down to the surface to the Mars Base and join our Mars Base friends Sergeant Bishop and his wife and family and check everything out. But tell them everything looks great. (Lieutenant Courtney) Sir, we have a communiqué from Earth It's the President sir. He wants me to put him on the loudspeaker sir. (Admiral Benson) Ok put him on intercom Lieutenant. Yes Mr. President this is Admiral Benson can you hear me sir. (The President Of the United States of America) Yes Admiral I just wanted to congratulate you and your crew on a wonderful job. Now it looks like we just might have another planet to live on thanks to you and your crew. Then Admiral said no sir, Captain Braymer designed and coordinated the whole project sir. (The President) Captain Braymer, you have done a great job sir. What you and the crew of Lunar Base 1 did was nothing short of incredible. I can't believe what you have accomplished. Well anyway all of you and especially you Captain. Congratulations, in one day all of you went down into the history books. Well-done Captain. Go with God Lunar Base 1. The Admiral replied, thank you Mr. President, God Bless you to sir. (Lieutenant Courtney) Transmission over Admiral. (Admiral Benson) Ok I'm going to my quarters. Commander Craft take command of the bridge. Commander Craft answered, Yes sir. (Admiral Benson) I'll see everybody at 20:00 at the party in D-104 the Red Star lounge. Great job everyone. Well-done Captain. Thank you sir. Then the Admiral left and went to his quarters. Soon everyone else started clearing the bridge and going to his or her quarters except for a few. Captain Braymer stayed a little while longer and studied the surface of Mars. Captain Braymer just kept staring at Mars and how the atmosphere was totally clouded, so thick that you couldn't see Mars surface anymore. There were storms everywhere, suddenly it hit him. I hope this doesn't cloud up the surface of Mars for hundreds of years.

Mars is still better off than the way it was. He found that there seems to be some Methane and Sulfur Dioxide gases. There was Nitrogen. He also found that there was more than enough Oxygen all over the planet now. It showed large amounts of water all over mars from all of the rain. And it was showing massive storms. It looked like giant gray hurricane like swirls with Lighting everywhere in the gray atmosphere. As he was looking at an x-ray of Mars he notice another huge cavity of ice deep in the core of Mars that was not affected. David was thinking, maybe we need to heat this cavity up and put the water back on the surface of Mars. Oh well maybe I need to call it quits until tomorrow. Can't do it all at once. Then David left and went to his quarters to get something to eat and some rest before the party at 20:00. Now on another note, when the Admiral arrived back to his quarters he checked his private phone messages. He saw that he had two messages. One from the President and one from NASA. It was Bud Walker. Computer, play the Presidents message. (Computer) Affirmative, the President came on his view screen, Admiral I knew you would want to hear this as soon as possible, so here it is. We just closed a big trade deal on five Powleen ships and one of them is a moon ship like the Galumpa just a little bit older and the other four ships are all different looking. But all of them have light speed capability. I'm sending up the design layout of all the ships, you're going to love it. Admiral Benson you get to pick the one you want first before anyone else. I'm going to go ahead and go. Give me a communiqué as soon as you can. I'll be looking forward to your communiqué Admiral, see you later.

Then Admiral Benson said, computer contact the President of the United States. (Computer) Affirmative. (The President) Hello Admiral how's everything? (Admiral Benson) Hello Mr. President. I seen your message sir. I contacted you as soon as I could sir. Mr. President as you know this has been an incredible day with the genesis of Mars and now I get a new ship that's thousands of years more advanced than anything we ever had. That is the best present ever sir. How long before we get possession of the ships sir? The President answered. Well as soon as you decide which ship you want they will deliver it to your location and you can take possession. They will bring the other four ships to Earth. You will have to put someone in charge of the

Lunar Base 1 and make you a skeleton crew to help you familiarizing yourself with your new ship with light speed capability. Also Admiral I'm leaving you in charge of picking your Captains for the other ships and they can pick their crew. By the way Admiral great job on the Mars genesis. It's just fantastic, I just wish it would all clear up soon. (Admiral Benson) Well sir it really was mostly Captain Braymer's Idea and he should get most of the credit. He's a good man sir, I'm lucky to have him and I'm putting him down for a commendation to sir. Then the President said, well I'll approve it Admiral. Ok Admiral I'm going to go celebrate with everybody here, I recommend you do the same for it is a time to celebrate. I believe I will do that sir, the Admiral replied. This is all so incredible. Well thanks for everything Mr. President, I am going to go ahead and let you go sir. We will be talking to you soon sir. I'm going to go through all the different ships, so I can pick one as soon as possible. I can't believe we will finally have light speed capability. Well, once again thanks for everything sir. I'll talk to you later Admiral. Then the Admiral said, computer end transmission. (Computer) Affirmative. (Admiral Benson) Computer put the layouts of all five space craft sent by NASA on my monitor and contact Bud Walker at NASA for a communiqué. (Computer) Affirmative. (Bud Walker) Hello Admiral Benson, how's it going out there in the heavens? Oh pretty good the Admiral replied. I was looking at my messages and I seen you called. Then Bud Walker said, we were monitoring your experiment on the Mars genesis. I just wanted to congratulate you on Mars sir. That's incredible Admiral. I can't wait for all the fog to settle so we can see the new mars. It all seems so unbelievable. Yes I know what you mean The Admiral said. It was Captain Braymer who was the project head.

He designed and coordinated the whole project. I am so glad you told him about the job and us. He's a good man. I feel so lucky to have him as 1st Science Officer. Yes I know he is a good man, Bud replied. Also I sent all of the layouts of the new five ships from the Powleens. I've already looked them over and these ships have everything you would ever want in a space ship. They all have light speed. The moon ship is huge it's as big as a small city. It's ten kilometers in diameter and it has over 1000 weapons on it all over the ship. They also have magnetically charged shields, we don't know how they work yet but we are going to put these shields on all of the Lunar Base ships. The moon ship can house up to 35,000 people. The other four ships are a third of the size but they are way advanced to anything we have. The moon ship and the Kawaka ship are some of their newest ships and they are way advanced from the other ships. They even left their weapons in the ship. I know you're going to have a lot of fun checking them out. Two of the other ships are cargo ships with light speed and they look like there's a lot of room on them too. They come with three shuttlecrafts each and they look well equipped.

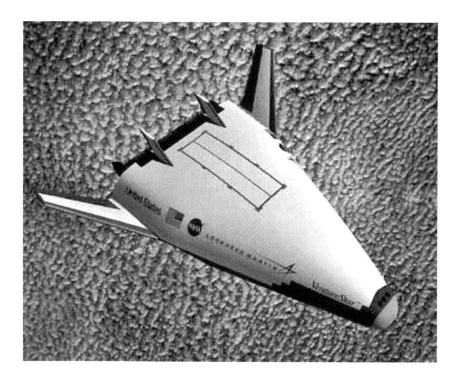

They have weapons too. The last ship is one of their standard battle cruisers. It's called the Remonda and it's got a really neat look to it. The Kawaka ship is the best of all of them it's one of their latest ships to date. They say the Moon ship that looks like the Galumpa is coming in a close second. Well Admiral what do you think. Admiral Benson answered, I can't wait to see these ships up close and personal.

Well Bud I'm going to go ahead and go so I can look at all of the layouts of these ships. So I can pick one of them. Thanks for all your help Bud. I'll see you later. Everyone take care. All right you take care up there in the heavens too. Then Bud said good-bye. Computer end Communiqué. After Bud Walkers conversation the Admiral started looking at all of the layouts of the Powleens ships. He started going over every detail of all the ships with a fine toothcomb. He wanted the best of all of the ships. Now over in Captain Braymer's quarters. David was on his computer analyzing data on the Mars surface. Planets rotation speed has increased 3 more kilometers per hour but is now steady and very stable. Core temperature is steady. Mars magnetic field has increased a little more since I last looked at it. It jumped to 53%. Mar's magnetic field is now stronger than earths by 2 %. Oxygen levels way above normal. Everything is looking great! Mars is still showing a lot of storms on the surface. It looks like giant swirls of gray and a lot of lightning in the clouds too. Mars Base has checked in. It has been very windy with winds in excess of 200 miles and hour. Their base is built to withstand 400 mile an hour winds.

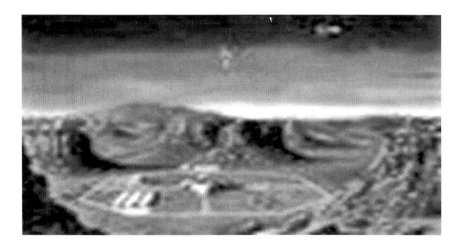

It's been real rough for them but their ok. A huge storm just past them. Maybe if we heat up the other big ice cavity under Mars surface deep inside the crust we can put more water on the surface by steaming it in the atmosphere and then it would rain down on to the surface of

Mars. It could also release more poisonous gases in the air too. God I hope this clears up soon. It appears to be mostly steam so maybe it won't take too long to clear. We will just have to let the sun do its work. Oh well maybe I should get something to eat and get some rest like the Admiral said and go to that party at 20:00.

David told his computer to monitor the planet Mars surface for any change in the magnetic field and rotation speed and clarity of the planet's surface. Then David also asks the computer to order him a shrimp and fish diner. Within 5 minutes he was eating his diner and it wasn't half bad. After he ate he told the computer to wake him up in two hours and laid down for a short nap. The Admiral back in his quarters instead of resting he was going over all the schematics of the ships. He really liked the Kawaka ship. It had a very elegant look about it. It also had so many other extras, it could house 5500 people. All of the ships were powered by their version of a nuclear reactor engine. The kawaka ship also had three shuttles and they were all the latest designs of the Powleens shuttles. The Admiral couldn't make up his mind between the Moon ship and the Kawaka Ship. The Moon ship was so huge and it had weapons all over it. It had a thousand weapons all around the ship. It also had many other things the Kawaka ship didn't have because it was so huge it had everything a small city has and more. All of the ships had their light speed but it did show that the Kawaka ship was the newest and the fastest. It also had a couple of weapons the moon ship didn't have. It had a new disrupter beam weapon and a pulse weapon that looked very interesting. They had primary shields and secondary emergency shields in case of a hull breach. The Admiral was thinking I guess the Powleens really are not that scared if we have their weapons because they have a hundred times the fleet we have and we really just have the three Lunar Base ships and these five Powleen ships. We are so lucky we made friends with the Powleens. Now we will have a descent space fleet and light speed capability. I wonder where we will want to go first. I still can't get over all of this. I believe I'm going to take the Kawaka ship. Well its almost time for the party I'll eat after the party so I can relax afterwards. So the Admiral got cleaned up and headed for the party. As the Admiral arrived at the Red Star lounge he noticed almost everyone was already there having fun except Captain Braymer. Then suddenly Captain Braymer walked in. Admiral Benson yelled out loud, hey there he is. How's it going Captain? Oh pretty good sir, Captain Braymer replied. I just thought I would come down and relax a little bit. Then Admiral Benson said, well you deserve it Captain. That was incredible what you did today Captain. I was so proud to be a part of it. I can't wait to start colonizing Mars. I'm giving you a commendation for this one Captain. You earned it.

I'm buying all the drinks for you sir and anything else you want, you just go ahead and enjoy. Everyone lets toast one for Captain Braymer and his Mars genesis. Everyone raised their glasses and said hip hip hurray for Captain Braymer. Everyone downed his or her drink. Then the very beautiful Lieutenant Courtney who is one of the many of the officers aids. Walked over to Captain Braymer and gave him a very long passionate kiss. When she stopped, everyone was shouting and applauding. Captain Braymer was so embarrassed and turned as red as an apple. He told everyone thank you, but he couldn't have done it without everybody else's help. He was also going to see if everyone aboard the Lunar Base 1 would get a metal or a special patch for his or her uniform for helping. Captain Braymer looked over at Admiral Benson. Admiral Benson gave a nod of approval and everyone just started to applaud and shout again. After everyone was celebrating for about one half of an hour and having a buzz and everyone into what they were talking about. Suddenly they started losing gravity. Then everyone started to float. After that everybody was real quiet. Then Captain Braymer pushed the button on his uniform and said bridge. The bridge answered back to the Captain. Captain Braymer told the bridge that they have lost gravity in the Red Star lounge. Then he said everyone is floating around with a smile on his face. Everybody started laughing and then asked how was everything on the bridge. The bridge reported back that everything's ok up here and that you should go back to normal any second now. Everyone was pushing off of the ceiling to go back towards the floor so when they regained gravity they wouldn't fall far. Then suddenly everyone dropped to the floor laughing and some of them got wet from their drinks that they were drinking. Then everyone just wouldn't stop laughing. The party went very well after that. Everyone celebrated for a couple of hours. Everybody got pleasantly buzzed before they started clearing out, going back to their quarters. The Admiral was one of the first to leave. It was right after losing gravity. Then about twenty minutes later Captain Braymer left and went back to his home. The first thing he did was get on his computer and check the surface of Mars. Everything was still the same as it was before he went to the party. He was happy about it because he felt that was a good sign the planet was stable. David thought to himself, well why don't I check out what's on satellite T.V. Man I love all these channels. You get over 5000 channels up here.

If you can't find anything to watch you must be from another planet. Not to mention if you want a view from heaven. All you have to do is walk over to your dining area window. Or better yet you could go to the observatory where you're in a glass dome on top of the ship. Or you can access the observatory right from your 80-inch T.V. monitor. We can watch any sports event on Earth live. We got it all. David watched T.V. for a couple of hours, then he fell asleep about 23:30. About two minutes later the computer turned off the T.V. monitor. David was sleeping pretty well, until he was awakened by his computer wake up call Navy whistle. David was rubbing his eyes when his computer said Captain Braymer the wake up call was because, you ordered me to wake you up if there was any difference on the surface of Mars. David looked at the time and noticed that it was 0400. Yes you're right I know I did say that. Computer, turn on the view monitor and put Mars on the view screen. David started rubbing his eye's and sat up. Computer what is the difference on the planet? (Computer) The surface of the planet Mars is starting to clear by 30%. I also detect a large amount of new life forms that were not there previously. There is a small amount of water on the surface of Mars that was not there previously. Then David said life forms, are you sure? Computer do a systems check. (Computer) Affirmative, 30 seconds went by. Then the computer said, system check is complete. System is functioning at 100%. Are the life forms humanoid? The Computer answered negative, the life forms are all different shapes and sizes but do not appear to be humanoid. Except for the 23 humanoids on the Mars base there are no other human's on the planet.

CHAPTER 2

The Past Comes To Present

COMPUTER WILL YOU put the location of the life forms on my T.V. monitor? (Computer) Affirmative. Then David said wow, the surface is clearing up. It's starting to look a lot like Earth now. There are lakes and some rivers. The experiment is a total success. Ok, there's where the computer is showing the life forms. These life forms must of came to life when we defrosted the ice deep underground. How could they have survived all of these years frozen in the ice? Computer, zoom in as much as you can on the life forms. (Computer) Affirmative. I still can't see anything, David replied.

If Mars is clearing up this fast it should be totally cleared in another 24 hours. Then we will know what the life forms are and we will also know if we should hit the other ice cavity deep underground with the microwave beam or wait. Man I can't wait for everyone to see this. This worked better than I ever thought it would. Well I might as well get up and get dressed, get a cup of coffee and then go to the bridge. David made him some coffee and headed for the bridge. On the way to the bridge he saw Lieutenant Courtney. He gave her a big smile and said, how are you feeling this morning after that party.

Lieutenant Courtney gave back the sexiest smile and said forgive me Captain I have a little bit of a hangover. David said here try some of this coffee. Oh if you don't mind I believe I will. Lieutenant Courtney replied. Mmm that is good, she took one more drink, Mmm thank you I sure needed that. You like your coffee like I like mine. You know I had a pretty fun time last night. I believe I had a little too much to drink though and I'm paying for it now. But it was sure fun when I gave you that kiss. David turned a little red, smiled and said you know I really liked that a lot too. Then David said, why don't we get together again maybe watch a movie. Or first eat a nice dinner and then watch a movie? Lieutenant Courtney answered, sure I would like that a lot. Most of the time I'm by myself and it gets lonely up here. You can't really enjoy yourself when you're by yourself watching T. V. Then David said, yes I know that's the same way with me. I was just starting to get to know a woman on earth right before I left earth. That was back on Halloween of last year. It's now March 14, 2049, it seems so long ago. Oh we still talk from time to time but that's really not the same. Oh please forgive me I'm starting to babble. Oh no don't worry about it Heather said. I know exactly what you're talking about. I did just about the same thing you did. I started a relationship with a man before I left. We do talk to each other sometimes but it's not the same way out here and all. I guess what I mean is we could die at any time way out here and I do get nervous at times. I would like to be with someone even if it's just to play cards or something. Like I might get a little worried when we lose gravity and start floating. When your alone it is a little scary but when you're with someone its fun. I have some friends but that's not the same though. So I know exactly what you're talking about. What's down on earth is down on earth. We left all that when we came up here and decided to do a ten year tour. Now we are millions of miles away and I don't think there's anything wrong with having more friends. Even in a sexual nature. Then she gave David a big smile and said, I would love to come to your place and have dinner and watch a movie with you. David smiled and said, you know we are a lot alike. When we are not on duty just call me David. The Lieutenant said ok, you can call me Heather any time. She was kidding and started laughing. Then David started laughing and said, how about at 1800 today. Heather gave David another big sexy smile and said, I would really like that. 1800 then. David said you have yourself a date.

Then she told David that she had to go the other direction and David gave her a peck on the cheek and said see you at 1800. Heather smiled again and said I can't wait, and turned around and headed to her station. Then David smiled a big smile and went on to work. David was thinking wow that's great it was getting so lonely and she is so nice and so pretty. It would be nice to eat and watch a movie with someone else for a change. Then David went down the hall and finally made it to the bridge. When he walked in Commander Tice said good morning Captain. How was that party last night? David smiled and looked at Commander Tice and said I had a lot of fun last night. I wish you could have been there Commander because I know you would have enjoyed it to. Then Commander Tice said, yes I know I wish I could have too sir, but you know how it is. Everyone has to do his or her duty. Yes I know what you mean Commander we all have to do are duty call. Well, did you know Commander this morning at about 0400 the computer was showing a lot of signs of life on the planet's surface. Really, Commander Tice asked, were they human? No David replied, not human but there sure were a lot of life signs. We will know more when the fog clears. Let me go and check out what Mars is doing now. Sure Captain, Commander Tice said, Also great job on your genesis! David said thank you and walked over to his station and started turning on all of its equipment. Commander Tice then said I can't get over how incredible Mars is looking. I still can't believe it. Keep up the good work Captain. David said thank you sir and started to check out Mars. He noticed that the Mars Base had sent a communiqué. They also confirmed the life signs and the clearing of the atmosphere on Mars. The planet's surface was about a third of the way clear. It was showing a lot of life signs probably about a hundred maybe a little more than that. Wow, this is fantastic! I still can't believe that I'm going to get credit for this. The man that brought Mars back to life again. Unbelievable! I can't wait to see what kind of life is coming back. Wow, they must have been indigenous to Mars a long time ago before Mars was destroyed. They probably were or they wouldn't be coming back now. Hmm. Maybe they were stuck in some form of hibernation when they froze. Well, no matter how hard I try I can't make it clear any faster than it is, no matter how much I want it to. I'm just going to have to wait. All of a sudden the bridge crew started to arrive. Lieutenant Parsons was walking with Lieutenant Fisher and Lieutenant Charles Courtney was flirting with them as they were arriving. Lieutenant Courtney was trying to set up a date with Lieutenant Fisher on the observatory. Lieutenant Fisher was laughing and she was saying I know what you want me up there for so you can make your move, ha ha. Lieutenant Courtney looked at her with a funny look on his face and said that's right how did you know? It's just that you are so sexy. I just can't help myself. Then Lieutenant Fisher said, well Lieutenant Courtney we all must maintain control. Lieutenant Courtney looked a little depressed or maybe it was the look of failure and then he said yes I know. Then Lieutenant Fisher started laughing and said, you didn't say what time you wanted to meet me there. Lieutenant Courtney perked up with an anxious look on his face and said, how about 2100 later on. Then Lieutenant Fisher was kidding around and said, maybe but now we have to work so get that dirty thought out of your mind and let's get to work. Lieutenant Courtney with a cute look on his face said, Yes Madam. Then everyone started getting settled in his or her stations and started to get to work.

Finally the Admiral strolled in and said good morning to everyone and sat down at his seat. Admiral Benson spoke up and said, I know we do not have mornings any more out here I just like saying it. Everyone said good morning sir. Right back to him. Everyone seemed ready for anything. Then the Admiral said well Captain how are we looking on Mars. Sir, I thought you would never ask. Are you ready for this sir? The Admiral smiled and said sure. Here goes the Captain said, at 0400 this very morning we've spotted over 100 new life forms on the planet's surface. Also Mars is starting to clear up at a very rapid rate sir. The Admiral just looked at the Captain with a stunned look on his face. Then he said a real long whaaat. I knew that would take your breath away Admiral. Then the Admiral Benson said. This is unbelievable Captain. Yes sir David replied. I know, I still can't wait for the fog to clear so we can see what kind of life we have. They are probably creatures that were indigenous to Mars before it was destroyed maybe stuck in some form of hibernation. Somehow they were protected from the heat of the massive meteor shower that bombarded Mars and then they were frozen solid and now they are defrosting and coming back to life again. I've been thinking Admiral we probably need to drop some food for all of the animals or we could lose everything that came back to life again and we need to do it as quickly as possible sir. The fog should be totally gone in about 24 hours, I hope. I suggest we drop the food then.

Then Admiral Benson said. You know Captain this just keeps getting better and better. I love being in on the beginning of all this. Captain as I'm looking at you I can tell that there's something more isn't there? David answered, yes sir there is. Now sir, I have found another huge ice cavity in the underground of Mars. If we do not have enough water on the surface of Mars now. We should be able to hit that cavity of ice with the microwave beam. It should do like before and place the water on the surface. It should give us more volume just in case the water on the surface now starts evaporating too quickly. Well-done Captain, the Admiral said. I can tell you are on this. Captain what you have accomplished here is nothing short of phenomenal. It's good to work with someone who knows what they are doing. Lieutenant Courtney call the kitchen and have them ready some food for a little over 100 animals. I know we may not have that much so just do the best you can without shorting us. Some vegetarian and some meat eaters. We will contact Earth and get them to send up a lot of food for 100 animals. Also get with maintenance to take the food to the cargo bay for the delivery to the surface of Mars. But we can't deliver it for another 12 hours. So just have it ready for then. Lieutenant Courtney looked at the Admiral a little funny and was wondering to himself. Do we have that much food for all the animals? Then said yes sir, and then sent the message. Now the Admiral said. I guess all we have to do is study Mars and wait until the fog clears. I agree sir, David replied. Then the Admiral said, Commander Tice I need you to take command of the bridge. I'm going to go to my office for a while. I should be back in a couple of hours if anything new or important pops up just give me a call. Yes sir, answered the Commander and then the Admiral left. When the Admiral made it to his office he started studying the schematics of the Kawaka ship and then the moon ship. He liked the Kawaka ship but he liked how huge the Moon ship was. His theory was the more room on board the more comfortable you would be over time. They all had long 10-year tours. You know I bet the crew would be more comfortable in the Moon ship. He started thinking why don't I ask the crew later. Then he just kept studying all of the schematics. I think maybe I would be more comfortable in the Moon ship. It's got so much more. It's got everything a small city would have. Hell, what am I saying it is a small city. 10 kilometers in diameter, that's incredible. You know that is pretty neat how you can pretend to be a Moon on some planet like the Powleens did us. Meanwhile you can study that particular solar system without being detected. I wonder where the first long distance journey will be. I can't wait to get light speed. We will be able to go to galaxies we could have never been able to go otherwise. I'll ask the crew which ship they would like to be in but I think we would be happier in the moon ship. There's just a lot more room on that baby. I like a lot of room way out here or way beyond in other galaxies. This Moon ship is so big, we're going to get lonely until we fill the void of no crew. Well I guess I'll go back to the bridge and see how everything on Mars looks. I still can't get over how successful the Captains experiment is. Now we have life on Mars. Unbelievable. The Admiral headed back to the bridge. Back on the bridge everybody was active and socializing. Lieutenant Courtney was playing around with Lieutenant Fisher. Lieutenant Fisher are you ready to go up to the observatory with me later? Why you want me up there so bad, the Lieutenant asked? Do you think you're going to score or something? She started laughing. Then Lieutenant Courtney said no not really. I just thought that we could get to know each other a little better. Also we can check out the observatory. I've been up there a lot. Lieutenant Fisher started laughing and said I bet you have.

Lieutenant Courtney laughed a little and said no it's not like that at all. I love going up there because it's a glass dome. When you're up there, it kind of feels like your standing on Earth because its glass from the floor up. Then Lieutenant Parson ask Captain Braymer do you ever go up there sir? Captain Braymer answered, yes I go up there every now and then but I haven't been up there in a couple of weeks. I've been too busy with the Mars genesis but yes I go up there. I like to turn off the lights so it's totally dark and then just watch out in space. I meditate on whatever problem I'm having. I too think it's pretty neat up there. I guess it's something different for everyone. Your right there Captain Lieutenant Fisher said. Lieutenant Courtney thinks its inspiration point. Everybody started laughing. Then Lieutenant Courtney said now you know that's not true. Then Lieutenant Fisher said, I don't know about that. You see we've talked to your sister. She tells us all kind of stuff about you. Both Lieutenant Fisher and Lieutenant Parsons gave Lieutenant Courtney a very funny look. Then Lieutenant Courtney said, now wait a minute she lies a lot about me to get even because I use to pull practical jokes on her a lot when we were little. I know I shouldn't have done some of the stuff I did but I was little too you know. I didn't know what I was doing. Why what did she say about me? Lieutenant Fisher was kind of blushing and smiling at the same time and said a long "Well" she told us how when you were little. She accidentally walked in on you when you were in the shower. Then Lieutenant Fisher started giggling. She then said you were doing some funny stuff in the shower, can you tell us what she meant by funny stuff. Both girls started laughing out loud and so did Captain Braymer. Then Captain Braymer said jokingly, you're in trouble now Lieutenant. Lieutenant Courtney was blushing and grinning and then said you can't believe her she's just saying that to get even with me. Then both girls said a real long surrrre. Then everybody started laughing again. Then all of the sudden a buzzer went off on Lieutenant Courtney's communication station. It was Bud Walker at NASA down on earth he was telling us that Admiral Baker and a few Powleens were just about to head out toward us with not one but two ships. The Kawaka and the Moon ship that looks like the Galumpa. I guess the idea is that Admiral Benson should look over both space ships and pick your new ship. Then Lieutenant Courtney said. Copy that N.A.S.A. What's their ETA, over? (N.A.S.A.) They're going to leave here within the hour. Once they do they should arrive in about 20 minutes after they leave here. Do you copy that Lunar Base 1? (LB1) Yes we copy that N.A.S.A. That's really something isn't it? We will be ready for them N.A.S.A, over and out. Lieutenant looked over at the girls and said wow our new ship is coming and smiled. Lieutenant Courtney then contacted Admiral Benson on his coat intercom and said Admiral, we just received a communiqué from N.A.S.A. Then the Admiral walked in the door of the bridge and said let's just talk Lieutenant. Yes sir the Lieutenant replied. Admiral we have just received a communiqué from N.A.S.A. Within the hour Admiral Baker will be here with a few of our Powleen friends. Sir they will be arriving in two different ships. One will be the Kawaka ship and the other will be the moon ship that resembles the Galumpa. Then the Admiral said, no kidding. Excellent Lieutenant I can't wait. Also this is not going to be just me. I will need you Lieutenant Courtney. Actually I will put Commander Tice in charge of the LB1 and take Commander Craft, Captain Braymer and you Lieutenant Parsons. Lieutenant Fisher you will take over the helm while we take a tour of two new spaceships when they arrive. Also Lieutenant Courtney you need to contact Dr. Moon and tell him that he has to participate in our tour. After we do our tour I will want your opinion on which ship you think might be the best choice for us. I must tell you though that I will have the last say but I do value your opinion. I haven't made up my mind yet but I'm leaning toward the Moon ship because it's got so much more. It's 10 kilometers in diameter. It has a lot more room, it's as big as a small city and the fact that it's a ten year tour. I think everyone would be more comfortable in the Moon ship. That's why I'm leaning toward the Moon ship. But I will be able to pick after we go over both ships in person. I also want everyone else to check out everything on the other two ships. Especially everything that's connected to what it is that you do in your field. Then I want everyone to give me their opinion on what ship they like the best and why. Now Admiral Baker will probably have his people already familiar with the two ships.

CHAPTER 3

Our New Home

THAT'S PROBABLY GOING to be the case. So we will want to stick with them and let them tell us how everything works. Also Lieutenant Courtney contact Engineering and Maintenance and tell them to send us a couple of men to study and learn about the other two ships. Lieutenant Courtney answered, yes sir. A couple of minutes went by and Lieutenant Courtney said Admiral we are receiving a communiqué from Admiral Baker. Patch it through to me Lieutenant, said the Admiral, yes sir. The channel is open sir. Admiral Benson spoke out loud, Hello Admiral Baker, how's everything going? I've been doing real well, said Admiral Baker. I'll be doing even better when you pick what ship you want because I get the one you don't want. Then Admiral Benson said, that's really great Admiral so I guess I had better make the right choice the first time. Admiral do you already have men that is familiar with both ships that can brief my men? Yes Admiral, Admiral Baker replied, and some of them will be going with you after you pick which ship you want as advisors. As soon as we leave here we will be there in about 20 minutes. I love this light drive and I know you're going to love it too. When we get there my men will get with your men or women and they can go off to whatever section they have to go and then we will talk about the two ships. I thought it would be best to first familiarize ourselves with one ship at a time and after we're familiarized we will take a test drive in one and then the other. Then we can talk about things for a while. Then I guess it will be up to you to pick your new home Admiral. Then Admiral Benson said, that all sounds great Admiral. It sounds like we have a busy day ahead of us sir. Admiral Baker answered, yes sir I agree. Admiral we will be leaving here in about 10 minutes and it should take us about 20 minutes to get to your location. We'll also talk about Mars when we get there. That's great what you have accomplished on Mars. It looks like we have another planet to inhabit. That's incredible just hearing me say the words. Well I will see you in a few Admiral.

(Admiral Benson) Copy that Admiral we will talk when you get here. Over and Out. Well people we have a lot of work to do. They will be leaving in about 10 minutes and here in another 20 minutes. So let's start getting ready. Commander Tice you're going to need to contact some replacements for everybody on the bridge. Everyone else let's get ready to go aboard two alien spaceships. We are going to have to learn everything we can in a very short time so we pick the right ship. But keep in mind what I said earlier. Then everyone started getting ready to go on board the other two ships. (Lieutenant Courtney) Admiral they have just left Earth. (Captain Braymer) Sir, I am tracking them all the way here. Their speed is incredible. Admiral I will put the two ships on the main viewer. They are going 200,000 kilometers per second. We should be able to see them on the main viewer. I will zoom in. When the Captain zoomed in on the two ships it just seemed to take the breath away from everybody there. Estimated time of arrival is 15 minutes sir. They watched them cut across the solar system at an amazing speed right at them. It was really fascinating to watch on the main viewer. A few minutes went by and then as they started to arrive. Captain Braymer spoke up, Sir they are slowing to stop and here they are. Then you seen two really bright flashes of light and the two massive space ships appeared. approaching them on impulse and finally stopped right next to the Lunar Base 1, within about 200 yards. It looked fantastic on the main viewer. The Kawaka ship is about the same size as the Lunar Base 1, but the Moon ship was huge. When everyone seen how big the massive ships were they realized that it was going to take a while. (Admiral Baker) This is the Kawaka to Lunar Base One do you copy. (LB1) Yes we copy you Kawaka, welcome to Mars. Admiral Baker answered, will you connect me to Admiral Benson Please? Admiral Benson spoke up, hello Admiral Baker how was your flight? It was unbelievable Admiral, Admiral Baker replied. It was the smoothest ride I ever had. I know when you take your first light speed run your going to think you're in a fantasy movie. You can't tell that you're going the speed of light but Admiral I know you're going to love every minute of it. I still can't believe we were just on Earth 20 minutes ago. I love it. Ok Admiral Benson we will send a shuttle to you to pick you and your crew up and bring everyone here. That's fine Admiral. I will hand you over to our Communications Officer Lieutenant Courtney. Thank you sir, hello Kawaka ship please tell your computer to dock your shuttle at docking bay number 9, do you copy. (Kawaka) Yes we copy that docking bay number 9. We have you locked in. We are proceeding to docking bay 9. Welcome to Lunar Base 1. (LB1) Roger that, we have you locked in for docking and will wait for your arrival. Ok is everybody ready to go to docking bay 9. I guess we're all ready, ok everybody lets go to docking bay number 9. Then they started walking to the docking bay.

Everyone was very excited. They couldn't wait to see inside the two alien space ships. They all made it to the docking bay and waited for their shuttle to dock. Kawaka shuttle was preparing to dock. It was a sharp looking shuttle. Then we heard Kawaka shuttle docking complete. Then the docking bay doors opened and the shuttle crew started loading everyone on board and it wasn't long when they were ready to depart the LB1 to go to the Kawaka ship first. This is the shuttle Kawaka waiting for permission to depart. (LB1) Permission granted, Gods speed shuttle Kawaka. Roger that LB1, we are now departing docking bay 9. Then they disengaged from LB1 and headed back to the Kawaka ship. As they approached the new and sheik style Kawaka ship they were so impressed with the view that they were awed. When they seen the Moon ship and 200 yards away right next to it was the Kawaka and you could also see how enormous Mars was, it just took your breath away. The Kawaka ship had its own tractor beam and as soon as we got close to the ship it came on and pulled us right into their docking bay and set us down as gentle as it could be. Then the huge docking Bay door closed slowly. Everyone unloaded off the shuttle looking intently at the docking bay area. Admiral Baker walked right over to Admiral Benson, welcome a board Admiral. How did you like the way the ship looks on the outside? The Admiral gave Admiral Baker an awed look and said it was the most beautiful thing I have ever seen. I still can't believe I get to pick one of these ships for mine. Admiral Baker said, yes sir and I get the one you don't want. As the two Admirals were talking everybody went off with his or her teachers to whatever section of the ship that they had to go to. Then Admiral Benson said which one would you like the most Admiral? Admiral Baker said I'm really open to either ship they both have light speed and both ships are on their own individual Computer a lot like the Lunar Base 1. It really doesn't matter to me. I like them both. I haven't tried any of the weapons yet but both ships have weapons all over them, North, South, East, and West the Kawaka ship has a pulse weapon and some kind of a disrupter beam, the Moon ship will soon have it. Admiral Benson I want you to meet Captain Dopar and his men. They have helped us out a lot on the two ships. They are very descent people. It would be my pleasure Admiral, Admiral Benson answered. They walked over to the three Powleen officers. (Admiral Baker) Captain Dopar I want you to meet Admiral Benson. He's the Commanding Officer aboard the Lunar Base 1. He gets to pick which ship he wants. Then Admiral Benson put his hand out for a handshake. Captain Dopar extended his hand out and they shook hands and the Admiral said it's an honor to meet another member of the Powleen people. Captain Dopar said thank you Admiral. It's an honor to meet you to Admiral Benson. They were very tall about 7 to 8 feet tall, in fact their bodies were elongated. They had a rough burnt skin look about them. (Admiral Baker) They have been advising us and teaching us everything there is to know about both ships in the last two months. You know we've learned a lot but I think it's going to take a long time to get to know these ships. There so big, especially the Moon ship, it is huge. I think you mainly have to get to know her as you go. Admiral lets go see the bridge and familiarize ourselves with it first and then I will take you on a complete tour of the Kawaka ship. It's a pretty good size ship. All of the rooms have high ceilings. I guess because they're so tall and all. There's one main elevator central in the ship and then you have run offs of the main elevator to each location. Everyone's quarters are also big and they have pretty good taste too. They have a lot of little extras. They're pretty classy you'll see I think you're going to love the Captain's Cabin. It's the most decked out of all the quarters. You'll see you'll love it. All though the other staterooms are pretty classy also, and roomy. As they arrived at the bridge the elevator door opened and Admiral Bensons jaw dropped, This is incredible, it so huge. It's three times bigger than the Lunar Base 1 Bridge. Admiral Baker started to laugh an said I had the same reaction Admiral. Wait till you see the Moon ships bridge it's twice as big as this. Admiral Benson said, really? Admiral Baker answered, oh yes but let's check this ship out first. You're going to love it. Over here is the Captains helm. David looked at his station and it was very elaborate. Their Main viewer was almost as big as the entire front wall. Everyone's station was also very nice. It had the Powleens latest technology all over the ship. We were finding out that the Powleens were a classy people. This was the Eldorado of all the spaceships. Admiral Baker took the Admiral all over the ship.

They went to Engineering and then they went to the hospital, they also went to one of the kitchens. Everybody even had a drink at the Powleens lounge on board and they were finding out that the powleens not only had taste like ours but they lived like us too. Now David went with a man by the name of science specialist Bob Parker. Specialist Parker had already translated the Powleens language to English on all the instruments at every station all over the ship. He went over everything there was at the Science station and the general knowledge and function of every station. David was very impressed. This ship was way advanced than anything we would ever have. It would have taken us century's to get us at the powleens level. The Kawaka ship was worth Billions of our Dollars. We really owe the Powleens a lot. They did more to help Earth than anything we ever did. David turned on the view screen at the station where he was so he could take a look at Mars from the Kawaka ship. He noticed that Mars was still clearing at a rapid rate but it would still need a little more time to defog. Mars was still showing a lot of life forms spreading out all over the surface of Mars of all shapes and sizes. Admiral Baker brought a lot of animal feed from Earth to distribute on the surface of Mars. But we still had to wait a little while before we can distribute all of the feed. This was all so over whelming and fantastic at the same time. David was in awe and said I can't believe we are going to get one of these ships! You are pretty lucky, replied Specialist Parker, not many people get a chance like this. Then Specialist Parker went ahead and took the Captain on the rest of the tour of the ship and after that everyone was to meet back in the shuttle bay lobby. Captain Braymer and Specialist Parker was the first to make it back to the docking bay lobby. As they came through two doors the Captain and the Specialist were going over everything that they had covered on the tour. As they were talking everybody started to arrive at the docking bay and finally in came the two Admirals and Captain Dopar the Powleens adviser and one of his men in deep discussion and so was everyone in the lobby. They were all so awed and excited. Then Admiral Benson said to everyone. Well how did you like the tour of the Kawaka? Everybody started to reply at the same time. We love it, everyone was so excited and the Admiral started laughing and said, Well People I will leave it up to you. We have been here for 4 and a half hours. Do you want to take the tour on the Moon ship now and finish up today or do you want to call it a day and go back to the LB1 and check on Mars? Captain Braymer spoke up and said, Admiral I just checked out the surface of mars on the bridge of the Kawaka and it is still defogging pretty good but it will still take about another 12 hours and the life forms are spreading out on the surface probably looking for food sir.

I suggest that we wait a little while longer about twelve hours and let Mars clear a little more then we can let the next shift drop the feed on surface where the life forms are. I'm go for the tour on the Moon ship if everyone else is.

If you want, we can grab some dinner and relax a little bit on board the Moon ship. We can stay on board tonight and check out the quarters.

Then Specialist Parker spoke up and said, sir both ships are fully stocked with food and supplies and fully fueled. Captain Braymer said, I'll stay if everyone else wants to. Everyone was so excited and said I'll stay the night too if everyone else wants too. Then the Admiral said, ok then we are all in agreement. We don't have to complete the Moon ship tour tonight.

We can do some of the tour, then do the rest in about 12 Hours after we all get some sleep. That sounds great Captain you have my vote. Ok then let's go to the Moon ship. They were all looking out the big docking bay window at the huge Moon ship just 200 yard away it looked so breath taking because Mars was behind the Moon ship. Then they all loaded on board the Kawaka shuttle. The big docking bay door opened and off they went. The minute they left from the docking bay on the Kawaka.

The Moon ship put its tracking beam on the shuttle and gently brought us to the Moon ship Docking Bay. Then a giant docking bay door opened on the Moon ship. It pulled us in and set us down in a massive size docking bay. It looked or reminded me of an airport on Earth it was so big.

There were two big docking bay doors. One that opened so we could come in and one door to seal the entire docking bay. After we came in the outside door shut behind us and then the inside door opened up to the docking bay area. It was easily the size of two-foot ball fields.

It went through the middle of the ship. It also had a railway system throughout the ship that everyone traveled to get to one place to another.

There wasn't a lot of crew yet, and it did look empty. There was what looked like a skeleton crew but not much more than that? There were even about ten neat looking fighter crafts. They all looked brand new. As everyone was unloading, Captain Dopar escorted Admiral Benson and the rest of the new crew to the main lobby where they took an air rail shuttle system to the bridge first so they could brief themselves and then go eat at one of the ships restaurant. Then they would go throughout the ship. Learning about each of the individual station for a couple of hours. Then they would go to whatever quarters they have already reserved for them. At the moment there was only one restaurant that was in operation on board the Moon ship. Because the Moon ship is 10 kilometers in diameter and we just have a skeleton crew on board presently. The restaurant they would be eating at was close to the docking bay and the bridge. The kitchen could also send you your meal to your room too.

But by going to the restaurant they could talk over everything that they were learning and see more of the ship. The railway cars that went through out the ship were very comfortable and also were very fast too. Everyone was really impressed. It was easy to tell the difference between the two ships and it was the size. The Moon ship was enormous. As they arrived at the bridge they saw how huge the bridge was. It was as big as two of the Kawaka bridges and the huge main viewer was all across the front wall. Hell the bridge looked like it was a shopping mall back on Earth and the main viewer looked like a drive in theater screen it was so big.

They talked for a while and checked out the bridge and then everyone headed to the restaurant where they all ate well. You could get anything there that you could order on Earth. Then everyone went to whatever station they were going to learn about. Well a couple of hours went by and then everyone went to their quarters in amazement. Stunned by the size of the ship and how advanced it was. Specialist Parker took David to the quarters assigned to him and showed David everything there was to know about his new place and how everything worked. They talked some more about the Moon ship and had a couple of beers. They watched the end of a football game on their satellite T.V. Specialist Parker was telling the Captain that everyone was going to meet on the bridge at 0600 and headed to his quarters.

As David was checking his new quarters out even more after Specialist Parker left, he noticed how nice it was. Hell they are just like us except for their size. They like luxury as much as we do. Some of the architecture was even more elaborate than ours. I think that the Admiral was right, I think the bigger Moon ship is better too.

David watched a little more of T.V. and then checked out the surface of Mars on the ship computer. David seen that it was still going to take more time for the planet to defog. Everything seemed to be changing colors from red to brown. What was clearing up looked great. Other than the planet having to defog, there was still a lot of storms on the surface. It's just going to have to take more time for the sun to do its thing. Maybe when I wake up tomorrow the storms will be totally settled on Mars, wow wouldn't that be cool. Then David turned off his computer and then went ahead and went to bed. He didn't have to worry about losing gravity on board this ship. It had it all. David was so tired that he went right to sleep.

Over in the Admirals quarters the Admiral was in deep thought about the ship he was going to pick. But he was pretty sure that he was going to pick the Moon ship though. The more he thought about it and the more he had seen the Moon ship the more he liked it better because of the massive size. He just felt that way, when we're off in some other Galaxy the bigger the ship the more comfortable it would be, and this ship was as big as a small city.

Hell it would be like taking a small city to another galaxy. I like that. Admiral Benson lying in his bed had made his choice. It was the Moon ship. He was going to listen to what everyone else was saying but he was pretty sure about his pick. Then the Admiral said computer. (Computer) Working. (Admiral Benson) Computer, turn on the view screen and focus on the planet Mars. Affirmative, the view screen came on. Mars looked a little clearer but it still had a lot of violent storms and a lot more clearing to go. Three quarters of the planet was still covered with gray stormy weather. Although the one third of Mars that was clear was looking really good, most of the red color was almost gone in what we could see. It was starting to look just like Earth. The computer was showing a few more life forms. Well it's still going to take more time. Maybe I should go to sleep and get a good night sleep. Oh I keep forgetting its day all the time out here. It's only been a few years since we started building the Lunar Bases in space. I guess I should've said another 8 hours sleep.

I still can't believe all of this and yet it's happening right in front of me. It all seems like a fantasy movie. Then the Admiral shut his eyes and he was out and 2 minutes later the view screen turned off by computer just like a butler. Everyone slept like a baby his or her first night on board. About 8 hours went by and the computer started waking everyone up and they started having coffee and breakfast. They all had to meet on the bridge at 0600 and it was 0500.

So they took their time and got ready for the meeting. David couldn't wait to check out the Moon ships Computer. Then David said computer. (Computer) Working. David said, turn on the view screen. (Computer) Affirmative. When the view screen came on he couldn't believe his eyes. Mars was about 75% clear and it looked a lot like Earth. It was a beautiful sight to see and he couldn't wait to show everyone else. There were lakes and rivers and normal looking thunder storms, it was literally coming back to life again. This is better than I ever expected. We lucked out and did the one thing that Mars needed to be reborn, and now Mars is alive again! Wow, there's even more life forms. About double what it was. This is so cool and I did it, Unbelievable! Then Specialist Parker came to David's quarters. David told Specialist Parker what he had seen on the view screen and Parker thought that it was incredible. They were both very excited about it and decided to head to the bridge.

They went to the end of the hallway and got on the shuttle car railway system. Before you know it they were at the bridge. As they were walking in, they noticed that they were not the only one's there. His Pilot and Copilot Lieutenant Fisher and Lieutenant Parsons was already on the bridge and they were laughing when they seen the Captain come in. They said good morning to David and specialist

Parker. David put a smile on his face and asked what are you guys laughing about? The Pilot Lieutenant Tawny Fisher said sir, we were laughing about the fact that Lieutenant Courtney had to go to the observatory all along last night.

Then David started laughing and said, oh yes I remember. I wouldn't hold that against him with a smile on his face. I think he's a pretty good guy. The two Lieutenants said oh we know we like him too. But I guess we were just having fun playing hard to get sir, and started laughing. David started laughing and said very good lady's keep up the good work. The girls both started laughing some more and said yes sir.

Now Specialist Parker was still relatively a young lad and some of the lady's might say that he was a very handsome man. Both of the Lieutenants were giving Parker quit a smile. Parker said to Lieutenant Fisher. Hi, I'm Specialist Parker I'm going to be a part of your crew from here on out. It's my job to show you all around the Moon ship. I know this ship pretty well so if you girls have any questions about the ship don't hesitate to call me. I will be your chaperone of the ship. I'm also on the computer. I would love to show you girls the entire ship. Both of them seemed very excited and said ok, we would love that too and started smiling real big. Then Parker said hey maybe you can bring Lieutenant Courtney along he sounds like a cool guy. I'll take everybody out to eat. We can watch a movie or something when you get moved in. Watching old movies was something everyone was into because of two reasons, one was there wasn't a whole lot to do.

The other reason was everybody had very large TV monitors in their homes. They just liked it like that, and it was the in thing. Then the girls said that sounds great. Suddenly the bridge door opened and in walked Admiral Benson and Admiral Baker, Captain Dopar, his assistant and also Dr. Moon. Everyone was in a deep discussion about the ship. It was all positive. The Admiral looked like he was in love and it was the Moon ship.

Then the Admiral said good morning to everyone. Then addressed everybody and said well ladies and gentlemen, this is the million dollar question. Which ship did you like the best? I want you all to be totally honest with me, that is very important. Lady's first.

Well they started with Lieutenant Fisher and basically they all said the same thing that the Admiral said. That the bigger the better it is. They all said they feel safer in the bigger ship too. Which made since. The Kawaka was by no means small but the Moon ship was enormous. Then the Admiral said well then it's unanimous. We chose the Moon ship if that's ok with you Admiral Baker? Yes it is. It doesn't really matter to me because one ship is newer and one ship is bigger either way we win. I can't wait to take possession of either one Admiral. Because after we take possession we will be headed to Pluto's moons. Then Admiral Benson said well sir, you are now the proud owner of the Kawaka ship. We are the proud owner of the Moon ship. It suddenly hit me, we have to name our new ship. Until we do we will just call her the Moon ship. Admiral Baker Thanked Admiral Benson and headed for his new ship the Kawaka.

He was in a hurry to exit the area and go on his mission. Then I guess we need to split the crews of the Lunar Base 1 for our new crew on board here. I'm going to put Commander Tice in command of the Lunar Base 1. Commander Craft can be my second in command on the Moon ship. Now then as of now why don't everyone go back to the LB1 and get ready for the move. Captain Braymer why don't you get back to your Mars project.

I know that's what you want to do anyway. For the day I really don't care where everyone works. Today it can be here or on the LB1 but for now why don't everybody go back that needs too. We will get everything in order. We need everyone's quarters to be assigned to them in a little while. We will get back in touch with everybody on this. Sometime within the next 4 hours.

CHAPTER 4

Meet Your New Neighbors

EVERYONE AGREED, SPECIALIST Parker told everybody that the shuttle would be leaving at 0900. Since we are the only shuttle this morning. They will not leave until everyone is ready that's going. Captain Braymer spoke up, Admiral have you seen the surface of Mars this morning? No I haven't. To be honest I was so busy with the picking of the Moon ship I plum forgot. Why what's it look like Captain? Well sir it looks better than anything I ever thought it would be. Sir, you have to see this for yourself. A view screen picture is a thousand words sir. Everyone was in suspense. David said computer turn on the main view screen and focus on the planet Mars. (Computer) Affirmative. That second the huge view screen came on. You could see that Mars was just like Earth now. Everyone was awed. They couldn't believe it and said a long "Wow." Then David said there are double the life forms to sir.

The Admiral's jaw dropped and said, that's incredible Captain. Then suddenly the Admiral receives a communiqué from Admiral Baker.

He said great job on Mars. Also the Admiral said he was ready to depart and wanted to say his farewell. Admiral Benson wished him good luck and off he went. He drifted away from our ships on half impulse and then you could see him pick up speed. Then one big flash of light and he was gone. You know Commander the Admiral said, every time I see that I fall in love. Captain did you check the air quality on the surface? (Captain Braymer) No sir, I was going to do that as soon as we got situated where ever we were going to work for the day sir. Very good Captain. Specialist Parker spoke up, ok everybody don't forget the shuttle will start transporting people from ship to ship about 0900 hours today. Then everyone talked a little while and headed to the docking bay lounge to wait to load. Specialist Parker was really getting to know Lieutenant Fisher and Lieutenant Parsons. They were all getting along really well. Finally they started loading the shuttle and headed back to the Lunar Base 1.

Once they arrived back David went right to the bridge. He seen everyone was watching the main viewer in awe. David went right over to his station and he turned on all of his instruments. There were several messages from the Mars Base. Everyone was very excited. They said the oxygen levels were more than good. Everybody was talking about all of the life forms. They were getting to anxious to go outside without air suits. We should do some more study's first. But I'm kind of anxious myself. So I really can't fault them. Let's get started. Lieutenant Courtney I need you to send a communiqué to the Mars Base. First tell them good morning from me. Then tell them to let me verify your data. Then if it looks good they can test their breathing outside the dome. I just want to make sure that there is not some kind of poisonous gas in the air that we do not know about. Very good sir, replied Lieutenant Courtney. Then David went at it. He didn't stop for a couple of hours. The air was showing that it was as clear and pure as our Earths, maybe even better. My God we did it. Lieutenant Courtney contact the shuttle bay. Tell them they can drop that food on the surface anytime they are ready. Then tell them to drop the food at the designated areas I have already picked out for them. Also tell them good luck. The Lieutenant answered, yes sir Captain. Also Lieutenant contact the Mars Base and put them on the main viewer. The main viewer came on and it was Major Becky Stevens and her associates. Hello Major, Captain Braymer said, I have been checking the stats and everything is looking great up here.

I will leave this call up to you. Thank you Captain the Major said, we have a volunteer right here. His name is Sergeant Mike Bishop he keeps joking saying that we always wanted him to be the Ginny pig because we don't like his cooking. David started laughing. I hope all of you are going to video this for historic archives. Yes sir answered the Major, we have a video inside and out. Sergeant Bishop was finishing putting on his air suit. They were putting his helmet on. Before you knew it he was in the pressure airlock room with his two helpers. Which is nothing more than saying the front door. Then out they went. He stood in front of the camera outside the dome. He checked all of his instruments. The two helpers were going to stand next to the Sergeant when he takes his helmet off. Sergeant Bishop said everything is showing nothing but beautiful Oxygen. Ok here goes, Mans first breath of air on Mars. He took his helmet off. Then he took a deep breath and said man this smells like fresh oxygen after a rain shower. This smells fantastic. Then he started taking off his oxygen suit. When he got done he said, see it's just like Earth now and laughed for joy. Then his buddy's took their suits off. Then everyone in the Dome came out without a suit and they left the airlock wide open. They were jumping all around and having fun and David was so amazed. Everyone on the bridge was shouting and celebrating. He couldn't believe that he was going to get credit for this. Boy I hope these things keep going our way. Now we can colonize Mars. Lieutenant Courtney give me ship to ship. I want to talk to Admiral Benson. Lieutenant Courtney answered, yes sir.

Admiral Benson said out loud. Yes Captain what can I do for you? Well sir David replied, have you heard the latest? Everyone was clowning around on the bridge. The Admiral could here all of the laughter. No Captain I was just talking to Captain Dopar about the ships. What's going on? Admiral you're really going to love what I'm about to tell you, David relied. The Admiral answered, oh yeah, what have you got going now Captain? What's everyone celebrating?

Well sir here goes, Admiral the Mars Base and I have just tested the air on Mars with live humans with no air suits.

Mars at this point is totally ready for colonization. Although most of the water has evaporated into the air, there is still enough to make it. If the rest of the water doesn't evaporate. I would still wait another 30 days or so. But we can still work now without oxygen suits. We will have to do more tests too sir.

All I'm thinking about sir is that what if we move a lot of people on Mars and it starts falling apart. I just want to keep that from happening Admiral. Then Admiral Benson said Captain this just keeps getting better and better. This is outstanding news Captain. You always seem to amaze me sir. You can call me anytime with news like this. I'm going to give you another Commendation Captain.

Captain I think you might have a promotion coming to. Thank you sir. No Captain you've earned it, thank you. Man when you do a project you don't mess around do you? David laughed and said thank you again sir, but we just got lucky on this one. I'm going to go back to my work now Admiral I just wanted to tell you what was going on. I'll catch you later sir. (Admiral Benson) Very good Captain. Then David went back to his work. He didn't stop for a few more hours. Then he decided to go and eat something and start packing for their new home. David hurried to his quarters and started packing and eats a great lunch. Before you know it his doorbell rang. When he opened the door he seen it was Lieutenant Heather Courtney. She was looking very pretty. She said I was in the area and seen you go in your place. I thought I would stop by and see you. I hope it's ok. David put a big smile on his face and said, oh it's ok all right. Let me say you are looking very pretty today. Heather smiled back and said, well I started thinking about that time the other day when we were at the elevator. We were talking about being lonely and how it would be a lot more better to spend time watching a movie or eat dinner together or both.

Well I was wondering if you mind being with me for a little while today. Maybe watch a movie or something? David said I would love that Heather. Please come on it. I was just thinking the same thing about how cool it would be to do something with someone. Or go out to eat with someone like we did back on Earth.

You know I left the Moon ship earlier and it is like a small city. It doesn't feel like a space ship at all because it is so big if you know what I mean. Are you one of the ones that are getting transferred to the Moon ship? No, I haven't made up my mind yet I guess because I haven't seen it yet. Or maybe it just scares me a little bit.

You know I sure did like that kiss you gave me at the elevator. It was a little one but it was a good one. David smiles and said you know really I liked that kiss a lot too. Would you like to do it again? Then Heather said, maybe we can make it a little longer this time? David leaned in and then they kissed passionately for about a minute.

Then Heather gave David a very erotic look and said MMM that was pretty nice what do you say we go and pick out a good movie. You can make us a couple of drinks and we can watch the movie. Maybe even do some more kissing and smiled. Who knows stranger you might just get lucky and smiled that sexy smile she has. She was a very attractive woman. She was also wearing a very sexy looking blue dress that was split on both sides attached with string on the sides.

David leaned in again and gave her another kiss and said lets go pick out a movie. They walked over to his sofa and sat down. David started to go over the movies with the computer. David said Heather you know, we've got just about any kind of movie you would want to watch. What am I saying, you're the one who showed me all of this stuff. When I first came on board four months ago. What kind of movie do you like Heather?

I bet you like Pirate movies. Well your right there Heather replied, but I'm kind of partial to the old movie Jaws. Do you like Jaws? David answered yes I do. I also like comedies. I like science fiction and horror, I love space movies. You know what else I like a lot Heather? What? I like the movie Jaws. David and Heather started laughing and kissed again. David said computer will you put on the movie Jaws please. Affirmative. The T.V. monitor came on and so did the movie Jaws. David looked at Heather and said "It's show time". Then they sat back close to each other and started to drink their drinks and watch their movie. The movie got to the point of Quinn telling his story about the Indianapolis and they started kissing some more and Heather asked if she could use the bathroom for a minute. David said ok but watch out we don't lose gravity boy the other day that happened to me. I almost didn't get the lid shut quickly enough and it was almost a nightmare. Heather started laughing and said, don't worry I'll be all right. She was in the bathroom for about 5 minutes and David was fixing them two more drinks. Heather came out of the bathroom and she was in the buff. Man she was a knock out. Then David said, wow you are so hot. Are you an Aquarius? Heather replied yes how did you know that? Well I'm an Astrologer also. You have a very sexy nature and I love that in a woman. I'm a Libra and we are very compatible. Then Heather said, you know smart men really turn me on.

She came over to David and then started kissing him and then they made love for about 2 hours. Somehow they had made it to the bedroom in all of the excitement.

Neither one of them had made love to anyone since they left earth and they were both really enjoying themselves. When they were done they were in a state of euphoria. David leaned over and kissed Heather again and said, that was incredible Heather, this has been a great time for me. What do you think about another movie?

We can pick another movie and I'll make a couple more drinks and we can still have some more fun watching this movie. Heather was lying on top of the red velvet sheets naked as a jaybird. She was absolutely the most beautiful sight that David had seen in a long time. She was a 10 for sure. Heather laying there on the bed on top of the sheets gave David a very sexy smile and said that sounds fantastic but before we do that, what do you say you come back to this bed and I will turn you on to no end. David started laughing and was looking at her lying on the bed and said I don't mind if I do. She had the perfect body and a wonderful personality. David felt he hit a gold mine. He was hoping that it was the beginning of a wonderful new friendship.

That's the way things pretty much was after the sexual revolution in 2034. When the courts no longer recognized sex as a binding force in a marriage. Men and women no longer felt hooked when they had sex to one another unless there was pregnancy. But that didn't happen much anymore because of a breakthrough in birth control. Sex was like sharing a super moment that they will remember for a long time. In another words sex did not bind you into marriage or a relationship except for a friendship unless you had children. Most of the time they gave equal joint custody for the children in a divorce. In these times sex was just like cementing a new friendship. Everyone just felt it was better this way. That way there was no binding agreements where nobody gets hurt in the end. Violence in marriage and divorce when way down. Since they cured all of the sexually transmitted diseases with DNA research back in 2030. Sex was also very safe now. Although they still had a lot of weddings, but not as many anymore.

Everyone just lived together until they didn't want to anymore. Heather and David made love some more. Suddenly as they were making love they lost gravity. They looked at each other and they started laughing and floating. But it didn't stop them one bit. They just kept making love while they were floating. The gravity was out for about 5 minutes and then they fell back on the bed laughing. They went at it some more until they were both worn out. Then they both just fell asleep.

One thing they did find out is that it is a blast to make love while you were floating. David was going to take the shuttle and stay on the Moon ship that night but instead Heather came over. He wasn't complaining because Heather was a super person. He also felt that this was the best way to say good-bye to the LB1 before he moved on. Maybe he could talk Heather into coming aboard the Moon ship. The next morning when they woke up by the navy whistle Heather and David woke up looking at one another. They both put the biggest smile on their faces. Heather said, you know I can change that Navy whistle to anything else if you want me to? I can make it say anything like, get up you fool your late or play your favorite song or anything really. David looked sad and said I won't need it after today because I will be moving on the Moon ship. Why don't you move to the moon ship too? I think you'll like it better because its huge, it's like a small city. There's so much more to do over there. It doesn't feel like a spaceship, it feels more comfortable and you don't have to worry about losing gravity either. (Heather) I didn't really mind the losing of gravity part yesterday, did you? David smiled and said no I really liked that, was it just me or did it seem to turn us on more when we were floating? It felt really cool to me. (Heather) Yes, I know what you mean. It did feel different and better somehow. I know I can't wait to do it again. Heather gave David the sexiest smile. David smiled back at Heather and said me too. Why don't you come over with me this morning when I move my stuff. You can see if you like it or not over there? (Heather) Ok. I believe I will. If I do like it will it be a problem to get a transfer? (David) No, I don't see where there might be a problem because the way the Admiral was talking. He was pretty much open about it with us. But I'll make sure. I think they will probably go with what I will say. Because I am a Captain and I say it's ok. David smiled and started kissing Heather. Then they got up and got dressed. David called Maintenance to get the rest of his stuff to take to the Moon ship. Heather and David had their last breakfast on board the LB1. Then they headed to the shuttle bay to go to the Moon ship. When they arrived at the shuttle bay, there was a shuttle getting ready to depart in about 10 minutes. Although Heather was on board the Lunar Base 1 way before David was, it was her only flight in space from Earth to the LB1 like about everyone else. She was awed and a little more scared than everybody else. David noticed this and put his arm around Heather and said, don't worry we will be just fine. Then Heather smiled at David and seemed to calm down, and from then on she seemed more fascinated. Especially when the LB1 docking bay doors opened and off went the shuttle. Heather was totally stunned. Her eyes were wide open when she seen the Moon ship in real life out of the shuttle window. It was so huge. Then David said, it takes your breath away doesn't it. Heather replied you aren't kidding. Mars looks like another Earth and from here it is so huge and the Moon ship looks so cool from the outside of space looking in. They were only about two hundred yards away from the Moon ship. She still griped David's arm pretty good from time to time. But when the tractor beam grabbed on to them from outside of the Moon ship and the big docking bay doors opened. Then the tractor beam pulled them on in. After she seen how big the Moon ship docking bay airport was. It was smooth sailing all the way to the giant loading bay section. Where they were set down as gentle as can be. They were right next to the docking bay lounge. Then Heather said wow, that was one of the neatest things I've ever done in my entire life and I did it with you. Thank you for bringing me David. Your welcome honey. You know I only did this one time before you did. It still fascinates me especially when you see how big the Moon ship is from the outside of the ship in space, in this little shuttle. These shuttles are pretty good size. They can carry 100 people comfortably and cargo for about the same amount. Then David said why don't we go to the lounge and get a couple of drinks and maybe a snack. I'll call a friend of mine. Hopefully he will know where my new home is located. That sounds great David. David smiled and said, well how do you like it so far? (Heather) This is unbelievable. I have never seen anything like this in my wildest imagination. I guess I can tell you more though when I see the Quarters that you get. (David) Well said, that's exactly what I thought you would say. You are going to love these quarters because they are also big and classy. You know the average height of the Powleens is seven foot 2 inches. You know all of the rooms have real high ceilings. I'll tell you something else Heather. They may have as much or more architecture class in all of their designs than we do, everywhere on this ship. Just look in this docking bay lounge architecture when we get there. Like look over at the trim on the lounge doors. They made it to the lounge and went in and sat down. David ordered a couple drinks and then David pointed over at the trim over the doors. You see honey look how nice the architecture is.

It had a very classy look about it. Then suddenly guess who walked in, it was Lieutenant Parsons and Lieutenant Fisher. They were very excited and talking away. They immediately saw us and came over. Lieutenant Fisher and Lieutenant Parsons said hello Captain and Heather. How do you like our new home? Heather said I love it so far, but I don't really know yet because I just got here. Then David said, it looks like you ladies are having lots of fun. (Lieutenant Parsons) We sure are Captain we just left one of the stores. They have everything that Earth has it seems. The problem is sir, all of the big stores haven't opened yet because there's nobody here yet. We haven't had this much fun though in a long time. Just being able to walk all over the place makes it seem like being on earth. Then David said, let me introduce you to my friend Lieutenant Courtney. You don't have to Captain Tawny replied, we know Heather and her brother Chuck, hi Heather how's it going. (Heather) Hey you two, what are you guys up to? (Lieutenant Fisher) Gina and I have already moved over earlier and we were just checking out everything and having fun. Captain don't you know who her brother is? (David) Is it Lieutenant Courtney that's in communications on the bridge? Then Heather gave David a funny look and said, yes that's my brother and I'm really proud of him. (David) You know I was wondering that the other day on the bridge when they called out his name. I started thinking about you and I was wondering about that. Well, what do you know? It sure is a small galaxy isn't it? Yes Lady's me and my pretty new friend Heather had a great date last night. We had a lot of fun Heather replied. Then David gave Heather a sexy smile. Also David said I thought I would give Heather a tour of the Moon Ship in case she wants to transfer over here with us. We just arrived here from LB1. I also need to call and find out where my new place is. (Lieutenant Parsons) Don't worry sir, I'll call from my communicator it's tied in to the main computer. Me and tawny already put ours on our uniform. I'll check and find out for you on the ships computer, it is all on the same line just like the LB1 is. Computer. (Computer) working. What is the home location for Captain Braymer on board the Moon Ship? Working, Captain Braymer's address is North West section. Room A504.Address complete. (David) Hey, that was pretty easy. Well Heather what do you say we go take a look at my new place? Heather smiled and said that sounds great. Then the two Lieutenants said do you want us to show you where it is sir? If you don't mind, David said?

Lieutenant Parsons answered not at all sir, it will be my pleasure Captain. All of them drank a few drinks. Then they went to the air shuttle that went through out the ship. They were headed to David's new place.

When they arrived they went right in. All of the David's stuff from the LB1 was in the middle of the floor. Then everyone looked around the apartment with amazement. It was as big as three of the LB1 residents.

Then David said, I could get use to this. Heather said wow this is really nice, I had no Idea. Their just like us. Lieutenant Fisher said this looks like the White House living room. Well David I just made up my mind, Heather replied. I am moving over here. How do I go about doing this?

We will set it up now, said David. Then David called Specialist Parker and started talking with him. Before you know it they had her place and an address. It was close to David in the North West section. Her address was north west section A302. She couldn't wait to see her new place.

Lieutenant Fisher said I know, why don't Gina take Heather and show her, her new place. I will show you all there is to know about your place Captain. Then David looked at Heather and said, does that sound ok to you? Heather said that sounds great and leaned over and gave David a kiss and said thank you. David smiled and said for you Heather it's a pleasure. Then they went their way and Lieutenant Fisher showed David everything she knew about his place. Like how to use the computer and all about the kitchen and bathrooms. She even gave him some directions about the ship, what little she knew.

All of a sudden David gets a communiqué from Lieutenant Courtney. Captain Braymer we just received a communiqué from Mars Base sir. They would like you to contact them sir.

They also suggest you turn on your monitor and zoom in on the planet's surface sir. (David) Ok I'll do that Lieutenant also Lieutenant I also wanted to tell you that I am giving your sister a tour of the Moon ship and she seems to like it. She's off with Lieutenant Parsons now to look at her new place on the Moon ship. (Lieutenant Charles Courtney) Really sir. That's pretty cool sir. I have been trying to get her to go check out the Moon ship myself and I couldn't get her to do it. She was a little scared of change. I have wanted to transfer myself to the Moon ship but I didn't want to leave her here along.

Now I can pick a place on the Moon ship too. Thanks sir, you just made my day. (David) My pleasure Lieutenant. I just wanted to let you know what was going on. One more thing. I was wondering if you minded if I dated your sister.

The reason why I ask is I went on a date with your sister yesterday. I didn't put it together that she was your sister. I was wondering if you minded me dating your sister? (Lieutenant Courtney) I don't mind at all sir. We made up our minds a long time ago that we weren't going to interfere with each other's relationships. Heck, we've double dated before. (David) That's great Lieutenant. She now lives in the Northwest section Room A302. I just wanted to let you know what was going on so have a good one Lieutenant. You to sir, don't forget about the Mars Base sir. Then David told the Computer to turn on the monitor and zoom in on the surface of Mars. Affirmative. Then the computer came on.

There was Mars and you could see the entire surface was growing green vegetation. This is wonderful. I can't believe how successful this Idea was. Look how beautiful Mars looks now it's got water and rivers and animals, now it's got vegetation. Computer, zoom in on some of the life forms.

Affirmative. Then the screen change and started to zoom in on something moving on the surface and finally it zoomed in on what looked like a funny looking horse. It was like a cross between a horse and a Giraffe. There were several different looking animals feeding on the food set there by the shuttle. Computer connect me with the Mars Base. (Computer) Affirmative.

Hello Captain Braymer this is Major Stevens, have you seen the new vegetation and the life forms on the surface? There's something even more fascinating than all that Captain. (David) You're kidding, what's that?

You're not going to believe this but here goes. We believe we have found about 25 humanoid life forms alive deep in the surface of Mars at approximately 25 N 45' 23" 94 E 02'34" We were about to go and check it out but I wanted to tell you what was going on. On the computer monitor it looks like the opening of a mountain cave. Is there anyone up there that may want to join us on an expedition? (David) Yes I would love to join you. How long do we have to get an exploration team going? (Major Stevens) Well Captain we are in no hurry so take however much time you need.

(David) I don't know at the moment how much time it will take everyone is getting themselves moved to the Moon ship. How about 2 hours? (Major Stevens) That will be fine Captain, just contact us when you're ready.

We will meet you at the cave location that I gave you ok? (David) Roger that Mars Base. Over and out. Then Lieutenant Fisher said wow Mars looks like Earth now. It's Beautiful. How long before we can move in, and now we found humanoids, Wow.

(David) We're going to do a lot of tests but if everything checks out we will be able to inhabit Mars in about 1 month. Computer connect me to Admiral Benson. Affirmative. Hello captain what can I do for you?

Well sir I've got some more great news and something a little urgent sir. Well let's hear what you have Captain. (Captain Braymer) Sir, Mars base has discovered 25 new humanoid life forms deep inside of the surface of Mars and they believe they might be alive sir. Mars Base is organizing an expedition team and they want us to join them and we need to organize an expedition team. We have two hours sir. We will meet on the location of the life forms sir. (Admiral Benson) That's fantastic Captain.

Do you want to join the expedition? (David) Yes sir, and I recommend taking Dr, Moon and a medical team and a couple of gentlemen from maintenance too sir. Then Admiral Benson said, very good Captain. Why don't you have Commander Craft go with you on the expedition? Yes sir answered David. Then Admiral Benson said Also Captain, Captain Dopar wants to join you is that all right? Yes sir David answered, it would be an honor sir. Admiral Benson said very good Captain.

Keep me informed as you go. Roger that sir David replied, we will all meet in the shuttle bay in the north west section in docking bay 14 in a hour and a half and I will keep you informed sir. (Admiral Benson) Alright Captain be careful, good luck.

Then David said thank you sir. They all met in the docking bay and before you knew it they were off to the surface of Mars. As they left the docking bay.

They noticed not only how cool the moon ship looked next to the LB1 but when everyone seen what Mars looked like now they were stunned on how beautiful Mars has become. It looked just like Earth with the vegetation but with a lot more land.

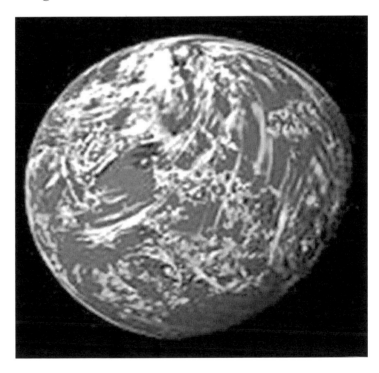

As they approached the surface they located Major Steven's shuttle at the heading they gave us. We set it down right next to their shuttle. Sergeant Bishop and his wife met us out side of the shuttle.

Everyone unloaded out of the shuttle and when they took a deep breath they noticed how fresh the air was. Then Major Stevens and their crew came over to meet them. They got to meet each other and everyone was commenting on how beautiful Mars was now. Then suddenly a little animal came close to the expedition and it was really cute. It looked like a relative of a Deer. But it had twice the color as our deer. We only have seen one Though. That seemed to worry everyone because it was so beautiful and cute.

Then Captain Braymer said don't worry we should be able to cross breed it with some of our Deer. We can also clone this animal to keep this breed pure and just change the sex with DNA gene structuring. Then everyone smiled and said way to go Captain. Then everyone headed to the cave opening. When they arrived there they had to move a lot of debris to get the cave open but they finally got through and into the cavern.

They found a path and they must have walked down that path about 5 miles into the surface of Mars. Then they came to what looked like an elevator door, but could not get in. Finally maintenance broke through the door using a laser. When they looked in, you could tell they were some kind of superior beings because of all of the lights on the electronics and the doorways. Everybody entered cautiously. Then they came up to a room where there were about thirty life support chambers with humanoids in side. All of the Electronics were on all of the life support chambers except one. Inside it, you could see a skeleton that had decomposed many years ago. In all of the other life support chambers that were on, the Martians looked alive. They had big heads and they were really skinning but they looked alive.

Dr. Moon and his staff started immediately trying to decipher the Martians language. Major Stevens and her staff, also Sergeant Bishop was practicing on the chamber that was inoperative. They worked on that for about an hour. And finally they thought they had it. Major Stevens told David that they were ready to try. Then all of a sudden another chamber shut off. You could tell that the Martian was dying.

Then David took a pipe that was on the floor and smashed the glass on the chamber and broke it. They immediately pulled the Martian out of the life support chamber and put him on a stretcher on the floor with oxygen and Dr. Moon went at it.

They believed that they had stabilized the Martian. Then they loaded him up on the shuttle and immediately took him to the LB1. Dr. Moon was not familiar with the Moon ship hospital yet. Dr. Moon left with the first shuttle and left his assistant Dr. Williams. Then David said wait a minute doesn't the Moon ship have a translator? The Powleens has translated thousand of species.

They might be familiar with this species. Captain Dopar said yes we do. I do not recognize this language but that doesn't mean we don't already have this species Language on computer. I'll call the moon ship and check.

Captain Dopar went over to one of the chambers and started talking to the Moon ship. Then he started shaking his head and said I think we have a similar match Captain. Captain Dopar then was talking over the writings on the life support chamber with the ship. Then he started pushing buttons and suddenly the chamber door opened. Then David helps Captain Dopar turn off each life support chamber and opened them up one at a time.

Let's get these Martians on a shuttle and get them back to the Lunar Base 1 so Dr. Moon can do his miracles, David replied. After they retrieved all of the body's they rushed them to the LB1. At least they were alive and that in itself is a miracle. Then Captain Braymer, Captain Dopar, Commander Craft, Major Stevens, Sergeant Bishop. Also what crew she had left to help transport the Martians to the LB1.They all went looking around inside the laboratory. There was water everywhere. Then they found the main computer. Captain Dopar started going through it deciphering everything and looking for information about what happened and who they were. They even found some weapons and they looked more advanced than ours. Commander Craft said let's take their weapons and secure them on the Moon ship. Then they found medicine in the hospital area. They also found a lot of frozen food. So they gathered up everything and immediately took it to the LB1. In case they need the medicine to save the Martians. Commander Craft and Captain Dopar stayed behind studying everything they could. They came up to a double door. When they opened it, to their amazement it had a lot more life support chambers of all sizes in it. You couldn't see what was in them but they were all different sizes. They were all lit up and appeared to be working too. Then Captain Dopar finds the last communiqué that the Martians made. Captain Braymer I believe I have found the last recorded message that the Martians made. Can you play it on the monitor, David asked? I believe so Captain, answered Captain Dopar. I just need a couple more minutes and maybe this will do it. Then Captain Dopar depressed a button, and suddenly the monitor came on. It was a Martian and he was a lot more healthy looking. He was not skinny. He was saying something but we couldn't tell what he was saying. I can decipher this Captain, but I need to take it back to the Moon ship and work on it for a couple of hours. Then all of a sudden all of the life support chambers started making noises and the lights were all flickering. Then they lit up inside of the chambers. You could see what was inside.

Everyone started looking in all of the life support chambers. Calling out what was in them. David looked in some and he noticed there were some children. A lot more people and more animals of all kinds. Then they realized what this was. It was a Noah's ark kind of a set up. They must have seen the meteor shower coming. They realized that they had to go deep in the underground to survive.

I wonder how long ago this was. Then Commander Craft called Admiral Benson. (Admiral Benson) Yes Commander. (Commander Craft) Sir we found what appears to be a Martians Noah's Ark kind of thing sir. We need you to send us about three more shuttles. Sir we found women and children and all kinds of different animals.

Sir we are going to need about twenty more helpers to sir. You got it Commander, Admiral Benson replied, consider them on their way. Once again, good work Commander. Then Commander Craft said, thank you sir. Captain Dopar lets not open these up until we get more help down here. Yes sir. Answered Captain Dopar. (Commander Craft) Well Captain Dopar, how do you think us humans do as a hole when it comes to things like this? (Captain Dopar) From what little I have learned from you so far I am very impressed. I'm finding that Earthlings are a lot like us with our values of life and in a lot of other areas too. In fact my home world is very impressed with what you did on Mars. We feel that we made the right decision by helping your world. I too am very impressed with your genesis of Mars. And I'm also impressed with this microwave beam you used on Mars. It worked very affectively. And finding these Martians is nothing short of remarkable. (Commander Craft) Thank you Captain Dopar we couldn't have done it without you. Earth loves your planet and your people and now that we can come visit. We can't wait to visit your world and celebrate everything that you've done for us. As they were talking the shuttles were starting to arrive at the base of the hill. They brought a lot of stretchers and oxygen with them. Then David looked at Major Stevens and Captain Dopar and said ok is everyone ready to start? Major if you and your assistant will start over on the other side, me and Captain Dopar will start here and we will meet in the middle. As they opened one life support at a time. First they would pull them out and then they would take them off on the stretcher until finally they met in the middle of the room. They were getting tired they went through 234 life support chambers. There were some weird looking creatures in the bunch. They found two hundred and three more Martians. Also thirty-one more animals of all kinds. Dr. Moon had to split the patients in half, he sent half to the LB1 and the other half went to the hospital on the Moon ship with Dr Williams. So far there were no casualties. They were still going at it for hours. But nobody minded in fact everyone was so excited about being able to breathe and move around without Oxygen suits.

David and Captain Dopar was ready to get back to their ship and let the next shift do their part. So they could get some rest and start all over again tomorrow. They were beat and so was everyone else that started from the beginning.

Major Stevens stayed behind with a couple of their crew and some helpers from the LB1 to keep on checking everything out. They had set up some tents down below the hill where the cave was at for the expedition. They had stored tents but they never figured they would be using them like this on Mars. They had also tested the water in a couple of locations. They found that there were small amounts of contaminants but nothing that couldn't be fixed or filtered out.

David and Captain Dopar headed for the next shuttle back to the ship with the patients. They didn't have to wait long before they were on their way. About 15 minutes later they were pulling in to the Moon ship-docking bay where Admiral Benson was waiting for David to arrive.

After they unloaded the Admiral walked over to talk to David. David and Captain Dopar told Admiral Benson about everything that transpired on Mars. They were all laughing and excited about everything. Then before you knew it David was in the air shuttle on the Moon ship. He was coming up to his north west section. Then the elevator door opened and he walked down the hall and behold he was at his quarters.

When David opened his door he seen a sight to behold it was Heather in a sexy blue negligee. I just wanted to thank you for all of your help earlier. I've moved in down the hall and I love it. I was also hoping that you weren't too tired. David put a big smile on his face and said you know this is the fantastic ending of a phenomenal day. You are a very beautiful woman. What more can I ask for. Then David leaned in and they started kissing. Before they knew it they were making love in the bedroom. They didn't stop for about an hour. David was kissing Heather and said you know I think I'm going to like this ship. This is the first full day on board the Moon ship and I already get to make love to a very beautiful woman. Why thank you Heather replied. What all happened down on Mars? (David) Well Heather check this out. When we first got down there we found 23 Martians in Life support chambers in one room that were in the process of getting ready to die. We freed all of them from the life support chambers. Then we sent them up to both ships.

There were so many of them. Then we hit the jack pot in another room, we also found what looks like a kind of Noah's ark situation. When the Martians new they were in a lot of trouble they started trying to save their race and some of the animals on Mars. By putting everyone and everything deep in the earth of Mars on life support. When the Meteors hit something went wrong and they were frozen solid for possibly 50,000 years. We will know more when they translate the language we found. Then Heather said Man, you did have quite a day. That all sound so incredible. (David) That reminds me I need to call the hospital and see how our new friends are doing. Computer connect me to the hospital information. (Computer) Affirmative. (Ship Hospital receptionist) Hello Captain Braymer this is Nurse Davis what can I do for you? (David) Yes Miss Davis, I'm calling you in reference to the Martians we brought aboard. I was wondering if you could tell me how they are doing. I was on the ground crew that helped bring them up here. (Nurse Davis) Well sir we have been very lucky so far we have had no Casualty's. So far everyone and everything you brought up is stabilizing nicely. Some of the first Martians that we brought up are even trying to communicate with us but they are much too weak. They all need rest and a lot of healthy food. We are anticipating a full recovery though for all of the Martians and the animals. Ok, that's the best news I've heard all day David replied. Thank you miss Davis you all are doing a great job. Keep up the good work. I'll call back every now and then to check up on our new friends. Thanks again. (Nurse Davis) You're very welcome Captain. We're just doing our jobs sir. I have total faith in all of you David said, thanks again. Computer end call. Wow, that's supper, no causality's, Unbelievable! We have been so lucky lately. It's hard to believe all of the great things that are happening right now and I'm getting credit for a lot of them. Well Heather I didn't realize it until now. I'm in the history books. I love this. Then Heather said, I hope things keep going our way. I am so proud of you David. Well honey David replied. I just got really lucky. I am a little worried because things have been going so smoothly. I have a feeling that something bad could happen eventually. I'm not going to start thinking negatively though. Hey what do you say we grab something to eat and watch a movie? (Heather) Oh, you didn't notice I had already made us dinner. David looked over at the table and he seen a candle light dinner already made up. You know you are my angel tonight.

(Heather) No David, you are my angel. I appreciate you talking me into coming over here. I was a little scared at first but now I'm not anymore. Then they started kissing again. Then David said what do you say we watch a space movie? (Heather) How about Star wars? (David) Ok that sounds great. I haven't watched that movie in a long time. (Heather) Well David it's show time again. They both started laughing. Then they went over to the dining table and ate the wonderful meal that Heather prepared. They had a couple more drinks and had a lot of fun watching the movie together. Finally both of them fell asleep and slept like a baby for about 7 hours.

The next morning David and Heather woke up to a song by Lean Rhymes, "Nothing better to do". When David woke up listening to the old country music he smiled and said I see you did some other things too. (Heather) I hope you don't mind? (David) No not at all. In fact I like it, I was going to change that on the LB1 but I never got around to it. I like your choice too, thank you. You know I believe the first thing I want to do is go to the hospital and check out the condition of our new friends and then talk to Major Stevens and see if they found anything else new. Then I should go get familiarized with my station on the Bridge. And maybe check the ship out and get to know her. What are you going to do today? Well I thought that I would go and get my new home situated, I have the last of my stuff coming. Then I was going to go and check out my new job and familiarize myself with that, and then I don't know after that. Both of them got up and got dressed, had breakfast. They gave each other a kiss and off they went each in their own direction. The Admiral had been busy learning everything there is to know about the Moon ship. The Next thing on the Admirals agenda was to name the ship. He had thought of a few names one of them being Apollo 1.

Another name was the Titan Moon 1, the Aurora, which was the Goddess of Dawn. I always liked the name Aurora. It just represents the start of a beautiful day. It's so positive. Well we'll all get together on this and we will pick a name.

The Admiral also wanted to go and take a look at all of the different animals that they had in the hospital. He especially wanted to go check out the Martians and see how they were doing. So the Admiral left the bridge and headed toward the hospital. Captain Braymer had just arrived at the hospital. He was checking everything out. Everyone was as busy as bee's.

David could see some of the Martians moving. But they were still moving slow and sluggish. Then David started checking out all of the patients and the animals. He started realizing the gravity of the circumstances. He couldn't believe that what they had done was resurrect another entire race of people. Not just the people but we resurrected another entire world and everything on it.

This is such a major success. They will be talking about this for centuries to come. This mission even impressed the Powleens. That makes me feel good because they might not regret trading all of these ships with us. We will probably be able to get more ships and technology down the road. Then Captain Dopar ran into Admiral Benson outside the hospital door. They started talking and when they came in the hospital, it was so big a lot bigger than the Lunar Base ones hospital. Everyone was rushing every which way.

There were only two hospitals on the Moon ship but they were as big as any hospital on Earth. This hospital was the equivalent of a ten-story building. It could hold up to one thousand patients. The Moon ship could hold up to 35 thousand people onboard. There was a hospital in the middle of the upper section, and there was one in the middle of the lower section in the center of the ship. We just had a skeleton crew and one hospital open at present. We probably had to go to Earth on our first mission to fill up all of the jobs onboard with crew and troops. David was in the middle of the hospital on the lower section checking out all of the different Animals. The Admiral and Captain Dopar was heading in the same direction. David couldn't believe how different the animals were from Earth. Some of them were really neat looking. They were also taking DNA of all of the Martians and the animals. So they could repair any damaged gene structure from being frozen for so long.

There were about fifty Powleens all over the Moon ship helping everyone familiarize themselves with the Moon ship. They were overly nice and peaceful and very intelligent. Actually everyone was really getting to like the Powleens. They were three Powleen doctors helping in this hospital.

You could tell they were all very good at what they were doing. In fact I don't think that anyone there would have minded at all if the

Powleens were they own personal doctors because they were so good. You could also tell that they were very excited about the Mars genesis and the resurrection of the Martian people.

They really were just like us. They looked like children in a candy store. But then so did everyone else. It was so nice to have all of this positive feedback. Then the Admiral and Captain Dopar seen David and smiled and walked over. The Admiral said checking out all your new friends Captain? Captain you are such a hard worker. Don't you ever sleep? Yes sir David replied. I was just checking the progress of our new friends. I am happy about all of them surviving. That in its self is a miracle. These people are so lucky they get a second chance in the universe. Captain Dopar said I brought a translator for the doctors and I also found out how old the Martians are. They date back to be over 120,000 years old. David said that's unbelievable. This is all so incredible. (Admiral Benson) It sure is Admiral Benson said, and you did it all. By the way Captain you are now a Commander. David's jaw dropped and said, I don't know what to say sir. Thank you sir. Then the Admiral said, no thank you Commander Braymer. Then the Admiral smiled and said you really did earn this. I don't give anything away. You should be proud Commander. I know I am. David smiled and said thanks again sir. You know I am very proud but not of me but for all of us. I couldn't have done it without all of everyone's help sir.

(Captain Dopar) Commander the Powleens are proud to be a part of your Mars genesis. I just wanted you to know that you are a famous Man on our planet now. David started laughing and said that's really cool. Thank you Captain but it really was everyone. Even you helped a lot and participated in this genesis. It was a joint planetary project and that's the way I look at it Captain. When I look around in this hospital I see a lot of hard working Powleens a long side with us Earthlings. And we all deserve credit. Commander the Powleens thank you but we believe that it was your destiny. You see we feel that you were already going to do it with the Lunar Base 1 and that we were very lucky to be here at this historic moment in time. In fact we are very honored to be your friends. From this moment on we are brothers in the destiny of our universe. When you found the Martians alive we were more than amazed we were awed. The Powleens rarely get awed but when we do we take notice. The Powleens had a very romantic way of looking at things. They were a beautiful race of people. They seemed perfect in every way. The Powleens were also a religious people. But it seems from watching and talking to them it appears that they are firm believers in Math and Numerology also.

From what I understand, it was numerology that helped them make up their mind on if they were going to do the trade deal with us with the ships. I am sure glad they did. We moved way into the future a thousand years with technology when they gave us those ships. Not only did we trade for ships, but we got all kinds of advanced gadgetry too from them. Food products, health advances that was a gift from God. They also believed in God and they have their own Christ figure. Which they call Gods son. Now we all know that Christ is real and known threw out the universe. Suddenly the Admiral received a Communiqué it was Major Stevens on Mars. Yes Major, what can I do for you? Hello Admiral I just wanted to tell you we found something I believe you might be interested in. (Admiral Benson) Oh really what's that? (Major Stevens) We found it in a back room behind a thick wall. It's what looks like a huge defensive weapon. It looks like it might be some kind of planetary defense weapon system against warring space ships. Then Admiral Benson said, this just gets more incredible every day we're here. There's always some amazing new discovery. This is fantastic it's like we're uncovering the history of our solar system from this Mars genesis. Captain oh I'm sorry Commander Braymer I need you to go to Mars and check out this weapon that Major Stevens found on Mars. Will you get Commander Craft to join you. Then Captain Dopar said Admiral permission to go with the landing party? (The Admiral) Permission granted Captain. If I had the power to give you a promotion. I would too Captain Dopar. (Captain Dopar) Thank you sir, it is an honor to serve you sir. I will give this translator to my Colleague Dr. Kopeck who was one of the Powleen Doctors and very good too. They were way ahead in medicine. We were learning a lot every day we were with them. They were literally angels sent from heaven. Admiral Benson said good luck and Captain Dopar and Commander Braymer started to go to the docking bay. The Admiral said one more thing keep me informed and then they left kind of quick. They were very excited, David called Commander Craft and they met in the docking Bay. Off they went to see this new weapon. It could put us way in advance in weaponry. Especially if the Arcons ever come back. We could also put one on Earth. This could really help us. Fifteen minutes later they were pulling up next to all of the shuttles parked below the hill. They unloaded and went in the cave at the top of the hill. Sergeant Bishop met them at the door and he took them to the weapon.

When they walked in the room they immediately saw a large kind of a gun barrel looking object about 50 yards long at a 45 degree angle and a large computer. There was a large box at the base of the weapon with all kinds of gadgetry on it. There was also water everywhere defrosting. Suddenly David realized what if this weapon turns on after it totally defrosts? Will it recognize our ships as enemy ships and open fire on them?

Commander Craft said wow your right. We can't have that so I suggest the first thing we do is find out how to turn this weapon on and off, preferably off first. Or how to override their computer. We want a weapon in here just in case it does turn on before we can turn it off. We also need to figure out a way to dismantle it in case someone tries to use it on us. Captain Dopar this will be up to you to do the translation. (Captain Dopar) Yes sir I will get right on it. Captain Dopar and Commander Braymer went at it for about an hour. Sergeant Bishop even helped. Commander Craft went back to the ship. David was learning a lot about the Martian language as they went. Then finally Captain Dopar believed that he had most of the answers.

The weapon seemed to be some kind of powerful pulse disrupter laser. They couldn't wait to try it. But they were going to secure it first. Back on the Moon ship in the hospital the fist Martian that they had recovered was starting to come around while a nurse was checking his status. Then the Martian panicked, and he had some kind of powerful mental powers. The nurse collapsed and the Martian tried to get up and then started to levitate above the bed. Then collapsed back on his bed and passed out cold.

Dr. Kopeck ran over and started helping the nurse that had collapsed. She was starting to come around and Dr. Kopeck put her in the bed next to the Martian. She was ok but drained of all energy. She needed food and bed rest. Then Dr. Kopeck realizes that they may have a problem and contacted Admiral Benson and told him. All of the Martians were starting to look better from being feed intravenously.

When the Admiral found out he put security guards all over through the hospital. Dr. Kopeck kept the translator near him and some tranquilizers at all times to give to the Martians, if they freak out again. Why don't we put a message on the translator that says don't be afraid we are your friends. We are only here to help you. We can also put it on the load speaker. That's what I will do. Back on Mars David notices what looks like a hidden door to another room.

As he looks closer he notices a button and presses it. The door slides open and low and behold it was a room full of hand held weapons. They had found the Martians armory. There was all these weapons lined up along all four walls in air tight cases and in the middle was a long casing full of small arms, they appear to be hand lasers. Very high tech but yet very slender. Then Commander Braymer walked over to the door and said Hey everyone you are not going to believe this. Then everyone looked over at David and walked over with curiosity on their faces. Then they looked in the room and seen all of the weapons. Everyone at once said wow, then Captain Dopar said look at all of the weapons. Everyone walked in and started checking out all the different weapons.

Then David said everyone be careful with these weapons we don't need any accidents. I know one thing the Admiral is going to love this. Ok, let's start loading all these weapons on board the shuttle. After about an hour and a half they were finished loading up the shuttle with all of the weapons. David told Sergeant Bishop that him and Captain Dopar were headed back to the Moon ship and that you can look for more rooms, there's no telling what else you will find here.

Everyday we are finding something new. The Powleens don't even have weapons like these. Captain Dopar said do you want to shoot one of the hand held laser? (David) Yes, I have been wanting to test fire one myself every since I found them. But I didn't want to do it inside the Laboratory. Well why don't we shoot the weapon over at that small hill about 300 yards away from anything?

They were over by the shuttle below the hill. David said Captain If you will do me the pleasure of grabbing that long rifle looking weapon. I will grab these two hand held weapons and we will just see how good they are.

Very good Commander replied the Captain. They grabbed the weapons and walked over to the other nearby hill. They started to try to figure out how the hand held weapons work. Ok let's look at this one first. It has what looks like four settings. David handed it to Captain Dopar and he was looking at the selector switch.

Commander if I remember the language right this should be safe and this is stun. I'm not sure what this means but I believe this means full power. So what do you say we try the safe first and then stun and see what it does.

David said you got it Captain, do you want to have the pleasure or do you want me to try it first. Why don't you do this one and I'll do the next one first? Ok Commander here goes. Captain Dopar aimed it at the base of the hill and said here goes. He pulls the lever down and nothing happened. Then he said, well safe works. Then he put the weapon on stun. He aimed it at the small rock and then pushed the button. Suddenly a blue laser shoots out of the hand held weapon. It didn't seem to do very much to the rock he was shooting. Wow, it still does something after all this time, 120,000 years old. I'm amazed it worked at all. It looks like the weapons are made out of some sort of supper hard plastic. So then he said let's change it to the kill level and see if it does anything, here goes. He aimed it at the same rock about the size of a basketball at the bottom of the hill. They were about 75 yards away from the rock. He fired and the laser was red now. Suddenly the rock disintegrated and they looked at each other kind of funny. David said very impressive. Then Captain Dopar said what do you say we see what this setting is here. Captain Dopar put it on the setting that he couldn't figure out what it was. Then said here goes, he aimed it at the place the rock use to be. Then he fired, it was a red beam but instead of being a defined beam it was a horizontal beam that spread out to give a large perimeter fire from east to west. Like a

140 degree spread or cone shaped beam. It was very powerful. Other little rocks started to disintegrate everywhere the red beam hit. They both looked at each other with respect of the weapon. Then David shot it next and then they went on to the next weapon.

They grabbed the other hand held weapon and it had four settings also. They found that it did about the same as the other hand held weapon. They did have a little kick to them, you had to hold it firmly or it could slip out of your hands. Now David picked up the rifle looking weapon and he noticed it had 6 settings on it. Captain Dopar looked at it and said I believe this means short and the last setting means long for distance. (David) Man you're handy to have around Captain. How long were you going to be a part of our crew? We have a one to five year commitment if you want me, said the Captain? Then David said If I want you, I wish you could be a part of the crew permanently.

I'm very impressed with you. In fact the Powleen people have been heaven sent to Earth as far as I'm concerned. I can't wait until I can go and visit your planet Captain, what's it like?

(Captain Dopar) We are pretty much like Earth. My planet is called Sybon. It is the fourth planet from the star An tares in the Constellation you call Scorpio. We are more of explorers and travelers than anything else. We have people all over the universe looking for ultimate wisdom about anything I guess. That's why we are so amazed with the genesis you have done here on Mars. We also get into trouble having fun just like you. We are pretty much the same really.

I found that that's the way it basically is all over the universe. Most worlds just want to better themselves. We usually do not have too much trouble meeting new worlds because most worlds want to prosper. The only problem we've encountered was with the Arcons and that was a misunderstanding that got out of hand. We weren't looking for trouble. We were looking to make friends like we did you but the Arcons were just paranoid and open fired on us. If we hadn't defended ourselves we would have been destroyed. The Arcons and the Thracians are from the constellation of Gamma Hydra, the Dragon. The Arcons are from the third planet from their star, and the Thracians are there neighbors on the second planet from the same star.

Then David pointed the weapon at the same place and fired it on stun, it was the same, a blue beam that didn't seem to do anything.

Then David put it on long range. He aimed it at the hill next to the hill they were at, at the base. Then he fired it at another rock about 1000 yards away. A strong defined red beam came out and was very accurate it went the entire distance. Then the rock disintegrated that he was aiming at.

You could have it on long range, on either kill, wide spread or on stun if you wanted. Or you could have it on short range either on stun, wide spread or kill. After Captain Dopar tried the last weapon. David and the Captain were very impressed. They left and took the weapons back to the Moon Ship. When David arrived back at the Moon ship the Admiral was waiting for him.

When David stepped out of the shuttle he walked over to the Admiral and said how are you today sir. I brought you another gift that I think you will like. The Admiral said, oh really what did you bring me now Commander? I stopped trying to figure out what you've found next. Then a couple of men from maintenance came over to Captain Dopar. He told them to start unloading all of the weapons and take them to the Armory. Then the Admiral over heard Captain Dopar and said to David, don't tell me, you brought me some futuristic Martian weapons from Mars? (David) Yes sir and we already tried them out and I know you are going to love them sir. (Admiral Benson) You know Commander you're like the son I never had when you bring me stuff like this. They started laughing and then the Admiral walked over to where the men were unloading the weapons and picked up the long rifle.

As he was looking at one, and he held it up. He looked down the sight and said Commander how do they shoot? (David) Well sir the hand held weapons has 4 positions on the weapon the first is safety, the second setting is stun, the third setting is a wide spread fire or perimeter fire. The fourth and final settings is disintegrate. (Admiral Benson) Excuse me Commander did I here you right? Did you say disintegrate? (David) Yes sir and it works good even at about 1000 yards. I know because I tried it myself sir. It's a miracle that they even work at all after all of this time. The rifle looking weapons sir, have 6 different positions. The other two positions are short and long range. We also found something else sir. You're kidding me the Admiral said, there's more? Yes sir David replied, we found what looks like a giant pulse laser for enemy invading ships or maybe to detour meteors. Sir Captain Dopar and I just disarmed it. (Admiral Benson) You know Commander I was thinking if there was one type of Noah project. I wonder if there are any more of these setups anywhere on Mars?

(David) Sir, It probably wouldn't be a bad Idea to put one of these big laser weapons on Earth sir. (Admiral Benson) Good Idea Commander, oh here Commander this is a list of names for the ship if you have any suggestions put them down on paper.

We will all take a look at them. Back in the hospital Dr.Moon and one of the Powleen doctors Dr. Kopeck were trying to communicate with one of the Martians that was coming around. The translator was working and the Martian was trying to communicate with the two doctors. Then all of a sudden the communicator started to work. The Martian was speaking English. The Martian was saying, what are you doing to us? Please don't hurt us. Who are you? Then Dr. Kopeck spoke into the translator to the Martian. We are here to save you and your people. We found you frozen in the Ice on Mars along with all of your people and some of your animals. I repeat we are here to help you only.

We are your friends. We are not going to hurt you. Everyone we found is in great shape for being so old. Then the Martian said something. Dr. Kopeck held the translator close to the Martians face.

My name is Venal Benish. I am the ruler of these people and of my planet. My planet is called Tirang. Please tell me how many of my people are still alive? Dr. Moon said we found in that one facility where you were at, we found a total of 226 people and 31 different animals that also survived.

Then the Martian struggled and said there are four more locations where there are more people and animals. I need to get up so I can help you find my people. Then Venal started to get up and Dr. Moon said, Wait and gently put him back down on the bed. You need lots of food and rest, don't worry we will find your people if it is possible we will save them. Please believe me we are only here to help you and your people. Venal was starting to look better. He kept trying to get up but he still needed a lot of help. Then Venal grabbed Dr. Kopecks arm and Venal asked how long have we been frozen?

(Dr. Kopeck) Sir you and your People have been frozen for over 75,000 of our years. We were told between 75,000 and 120,000 of our years old. Then Venal just looked at Dr. Moon and then he started looking around at everyone working hard to save all of his people. Then he looked at his arms and hands how sickly he looked, and how skinny he was and he gave a weird look and laid back down on the bed. Dr. Kopeck said to Venal, if I show you a picture of your world, would you try to show the location of the rest of your people? We will save them too, just like we are doing for you and your friends now. Dr. Kopeck then showed Venal a hand held electronic map of Mars and Venal started to point out the other four sights.

Dr. Kopeck was marking them as they went. After they were done Dr. Kopeck thanked Venal. He then immediately called the Admiral and told him about the other four sites on Mars. Where there were more people and more animals. The Admiral immediately set up four more shuttles on their way to four different locations with help to bring the rest of the Martians to the Moon ship. The first laboratory they found, what was left of it was totally wiped out.

A large meteor had slammed dead on and crushed it and it was now a giant crater. The second laboratory they found had some survivors but was also hit hard. There were only a few survivors, some people and some animals.

Now the third and fourth laboratories were found in tacked and they found over 570 more people and 300 more animals with some birds. We also found some plant life growing in the laboratory.

We were surmising that the animals that were on the planet when we thawed it out were somehow from the laboratories that didn't make it. We did find some dead animals that didn't survive the genesis but we have their DNA for cloning. When they finally got all of the Martian people and animals on board the LB1 and the Moon ship they were packed in the hospitals. Practically everyone on board was volunteering to help the hospitals out. The animals were the hardest to control. Nobody was figuring on finding all these people and animals. They also found more weapons. Each laboratory had its own giant disrupter laser which were all dismantled until further notice. We were eventually going to take two of the big weapons to Earth for Earth's defense. We decided to keep a lot of the animals on Mars in a Zoo like environment once they were totally revived. Just until we were able to clone a lot of them and mate them if possible. Maintenance was busy none stop making cages for some of the animals and some types of birds. So over all we were able to save 796 Martians, 410 men, 283 women and 103 children and 331 animals of all kinds. We also found plant life that was over 120,000 years old and a lot of medicines and some unknown chemicals. We knew we had to colonize Mars soon so we would have some homes for the Martians and everybody else. We also found enough weapons to arm everyone on board both the LB1 and the Moon ship together if they were fully staffed 2 times over. We had advanced in all of our weaponry in both ships. The way everyone was looking at it was that Mars was like salvage rights, if it wasn't for us doing the genesis they may not have ever have been brought back to life again or maybe not for another million years, who knows. Everyone felt that Mars was not only the property of the Martians first but we all felt that Mars was ours too. So we should be accepted when we start colonizing Mars at least that was the way everyone was looking at it.

CHAPTER 5

The Return of the Arcons

THE CREW FINALLY got together and voted on the new name of the Moon Ship and it was "the Aurora", "Goddess of the Dawn". Back on Earth everyone was filling out applications to staff the Aurora Moon ship. Those who were accepted were launched from Earth to the other ships orbiting Earth in space waiting for the Aurora to come back to Earth to pick them up, it was easier to do it that way. Then after that off they would go on a ten year tour on the Aurora. Some were military and some were civilians. The Admiral would have to leave Mars to go on his first flight on the Aurora and it's to Earth. They had to pick up the Aurora's crew, then return back to Mars. It would take about 2 weeks of loading all of the crew. Everyone will be starting to load the Aurora from the Lunar Base 2 and the other three Powleen ships orbiting Earth. As soon as the Aurora arrives back.

The Kawaka ship was close to Pluto studying its Moons. The Lunar base 3 was in route to Jupiter. It would be better to help the Martians on board with a full crew. We will leave some of the more critical Martian patients on Earth. Then when they get better we will bring them back to Mars. The President wanted to keep the Martians on or close to their own planet, so they wouldn't get frightened. They would get more attention that way too. Admiral Benson decided he was ready to go and pick up his crew. Maintenance had just completed disassembling two of the large laser weapons on Mars to take to Earth to set up for Earth defense. Finally they were prepared to leave and they pulled away from Mars on half impulse. When they reached a safe distance away they put the pedal to the metal and off they went. They went the speed of light and it was as smooth as butter even at that rate of speed they were going. As they arrived back at Earth 25 minutes later, they couldn't believe it. They slowed down well before they arrived at Earth and approached Earth on Impulse power. They parked right next to the smaller battle cruise ship called the Remonda, and one of the big cargo ships that they had gotten from the Powleens.

Most of the crew was mainly on them two ships. From space it looked like Earth had a second Moon.

Also on Earth now it looked like Mars was a second Earth with more land than water. The Admiral was not only realizing the power of the Aurora but also the advantage of having another planet like Mars to colonize. Admiral Benson was in a state of euphoria. Ironically speaking the Aurora seemed to really be the Goddess of the Dawn to the Admiral. A new space age for Earth, we could go anywhere in the universe and be there in a matter of weeks or months. It's always nice to know that we have friends out there like the Powleens to help us if we need it. Then all of the shuttles started to come to the Aurora. One after another, doing nothing but unloading people and luggage then escorting them to their new home on board the Aurora. They were also loading a lot of land base construction material. They only had to load about twenty thousand people in two weeks. It was the largest move to space ever. NASA was so busy, it was like the greyhound bus station. Everyone was so excited and happy. Most felt very lucky to get the Aurora for their ship because it was as big as a small city and it was mobile. You had to be a special kind of person to do this kind of stuff. You at least had to have adventure in your blood because everyday there was something new happening. Everyone was also excited about Mars. There were a lot of requests to move to Mars by private citizens. In fact there was a waiting list for both Mars and all of the new ships the Powleens traded us. Why they were at Earth, the Admiral went ahead and toured the other three Powleen ships in his fleet. He was very impressed with his new fleet. In fact he wanted to trade for more ships as soon as possible. The Admiral was going to go down to Earth but the Admiral was too excited and there was so much to do. They also took the new large land base weapons from Mars down to Earth and set them up using our computer systems to run it. Thanks to the Powleens they were able to translate everything into English. They put one in NORAD and they put the other one in Australia in Sidney. Everyone felt better, when we set the big guns up. We wanted to test them but was in no hurry so they thought. Eventually they were going to launch a dummy rocket and shoot it down. They were in no hurry, there was no need to at the moment everything was peaceful with no trouble what so ever. It was a great time in Earth's history. Everyone was filled with great hope for the future. After about a week they were way ahead of schedule. They were going to bring the last of the passengers and luggage up today and then the last of the supplies.

We even brought some of our plant life, also they had brought a lot of seeds of all kinds and some trees. They even brought some plankton and some fish. Soon they would head back to Mars. The Aurora had a lot of people come just to help and look at the Martians and their animals. Eventually we were going to bring some more of Earths animals and more fish but we had our cup full at the moment. Finally we were loaded and ready to return to Mars. Man we had a lot of goodies for Mars. The Aurora slowly took off on half impulse speed until they had a safe distance away from Earth and the other ships. Then off they went and with no problems what so ever. They arrived back to Mars in 30 minutes and parked right next to the LB1 on the other side of the ship. Well it wasn't long before they started to take all of the supplies and construction material down to the surface of Mars. Before you know it they were building homes everywhere and planting trees and seeds they were growing good in the Martian soil. You could see green all over Mars. It was a beautiful sight to see. The planets geophysical structure was very stable and sound. David always felt that they could have hit Mars with the microwave beam one more time on the other ice cavity deep in Mars crust. To put more water on the surface. David figured that they could always do it anytime they wanted later on down the road. It would be better to do it before colonization. A couple of weeks went by and the Martians were all getting healthier and looking a lot better. They were putting on some weight and were very happy. They couldn't wait to help with the rebuilding of Mars. We were finding out all about the Martians powers of levitating and mind control. They had telekinetic and telekinesis powers. They were very good at mental telepathies of all kinds. But they loved us and the Powleens for reviving them and their planet. It was like God gave them a second chance in the universe and they weren't going to forget it. They didn't mind at all us living with them in fact they wanted the Powleens and us to live with them on Mars. They were just happy to be alive again. They were way advanced to not only us but they were ahead of the Powleens also. They were the original caretakers of our solar system. They could teach us a lot about our past. It was nice to see the palm trees when they came to the Mars base because now when you land you see some building being erected and some trees and some vehicles running around you could tell it wasn't going to be long now before you start seeing cities and roads. It was fantastic.

Back on the Aurora, Admiral Benson was receiving a communiqué from Earth, it was the President. (Admiral Benson) Hello Mr. President, what can I do for you? (The President) How are you today Admiral, good I hope. I'm afraid I might have some bad news. (Admiral Benson) Oh really what's that? (The President) Well Admiral I have just received a communiqué from Sybon. It appears that the Arcons are on the warpath again. The Powleens have told me that they had another run in with the Arcons close to their solar system. The Arcons lost a couple more ships and they were saying a lot of threatening statements towards the Powleens. They do not think the Arcons will mesh with Earth but they said you never know what they are going to do. So they advised us to keep an eye open for possible trouble because of your new ships. (Admiral Benson) I knew things were starting to go too smoothly. Well thank you for the warning Mr. President we will keep an extra eye peeled for the Arcons. If we see anything we will give you a call. Thanks again sir. (The President) No Admiral, thank you, keep up the good work. (Admiral Benson) Thanks again sir. As soon as the communiqué was over, Admiral Benson contacted Commander Craft and Commander Tice who was in charge of the bridge at the time. He told him to keep an eye out for enemy ships in our solar system or close to it. If you spot anything out of the ordinary. Go ahead and put us on yellow alert. Also contact the LB1 and all of our fleet and tell them the same thing. (Commander Tice) Yes sir, I will get on it immediately sir. Was there a sighting somewhere sir? (Admiral Benson) Yes Commander there was. The Arcons attacked the Powleens and the Powleens had to destroy two more of their ships. They also made some threats that I hope we do not have anything to do with. (Commander Tice) Yes sir. I will get right on it sir. (Admiral Benson) Thank you Commander. The Admiral was concerned about the Arcons coming to our solar system. Because we destroyed one of their ships in the last battle. He was thinking, we just filled the ship up with crew. We should be better off with a full crew. I hope we don't have a lot of casualties if we go into battle with the Arcons. Then the Admiral started to think what if we put one of those Martian planetary guns on the Aurora it would be the strongest ship in the fleet. Then the Admiral contacted the Armory and was asking Lieutenant Welch an expert in Armament, if we could mount the Martian big gun on the Aurora.

Lieutenant Welch said they didn't see why they couldn't put one of the weapons on board in fact it wouldn't be that hard at all. The only thing I might be a little worried about is possibly a hard recoil but there is no way to know sir, without firing the weapon. So the Admiral said hum hard recoil. What are you saying? You mean it might push the ship backwards in space, or hurt the ship in some way. (Lieutenant Welch) Well sir, they had this weapon mounted on land. It might be nothing but there might have been a reason like recoil. We really need to test the weapon sir. (Admiral Benson) I agree Lieutenant, but we might not have the time. Go ahead and mount it on the Aurora. I will talk to Venal the leader of Mars about the recoil. (Lieutenant Welch) I'll get right on it sir. So the Admiral was thinking, Mars still has two big guns left. If we take one it will definitely help us if we encounter the Arcons. The Admiral did not know if Venal would approve of taking the planetary weapons to Earth or to put one on the Aurora.

He had to think of Earth because there are six billion people on Earth. That takes priority over Mars. Almost all of the Martians are up and walking around and they loved us for bringing them back to life again. We had started to learn a lot about our planet Earths history from the Martians. Venal the ruler of the Martians highly respected us and was a good ally. He was like watching his wife give birth to his baby boy. As he over seen what was going on with Mars. He was so excited. We were going to put him back in power on Mars jointly with us. The Admiral knew where Venal was. He was probably in the hospital helping all of his people. The Admiral contacted Venal and asked him if he didn't mind meeting with him about something that was important. Venal responded right away and said, yes Admiral where would you like to meet? The Admiral said the new Red Star lounge is right by the hospital. I was wondering if you could meet me there if that was ok? (Venal) Yes Admiral that is fine. The Admiral immediately left and went to meet Venal at the Red Star lounge. He arrive about 10 minutes later. Venal was already there waiting at a booth. So the Admiral walked over and shook the hand of Venal and sat down at the booth. (Admiral Benson) Thank you for meeting me on such short notice. I would not have asked you here if it wasn't important so please forgive me? Venal had a small translator on him that was found in Venal's laboratory. He started talking into it and said No problem Admiral how can I help you? (Admiral Benson) Well sir it's come to my attention that we might all have a serious problem coming our way. Our friends the Powleens have informed us of some possible trouble with some of our neighbors. You see this is kind of hard to explain but before we did the genesis on your planet. We had a run in with a species called the Arcons when we met the Powleens. The Arcons are a war like race and they attacked us unjustly. We had to defend ourselves in self-defense and we destroyed them. We did not want to fight them because we are a peaceful world. But I don't think that they cared. We have it all on our computer video. I suggest you look at the video when you get a chance and see for yourself what happened. Well the reason I ask you here is to talk to you about your big land base weapons. We disassembled them because we were worried about your computer coming on and attacking our ships, while we were rescuing your people. What we did was take two of them to Earth to protect Earth because we have six billion people there. We left the other two here. When we heard that the Arcons might be coming we put one of these big guns on the Aurora. I hope you do not mind but the Arcons out number us about 300 to 400 ships to 8 of our ships. On the bright side our friends the Powleens have told us that they will help us if we need it. But I thought we could protect your planet better if we put one of your planetary guns on our ship. (Venal) Admiral first of all, I thank you for saving not only my world but my people too. You are doing the right thing and I do not mind at all. In fact if you need our help with the Arcons you have our support. (Admiral Benson) Well sir, another reason why I ask you here was that our armament specialist was wondering, if you knew if putting your pulse laser on our ship would hurt us in any way when we fire it off the Aurora. (Venal) I believe because of the size of your Aurora ship that you should be all right. That weapon was set up because of constant meteors showers colliding into our world. There was another star in the region close to what you call Pluto further out in space in your solar system that went super nova. Then all of its pieces got caught up into the meteor belt that is now between us and what you call Jupiter. Then slung outward toward us. We were constantly getting bombarded with meteor showers the last two years of our existence. The last meteor shower was so immense that we could not defend ourselves. It was another meteor that hit the meteor belt, which sent the devastating meteor shower that destroyed my planet and almost all of my people. We had a population of about four billion people. We will never forget you resurrecting us.

We will always be your friends. As for the way your planet Earth started back in our time. Your Earth was mostly a hot molten lava with mostly volcanic activity.

There was no way at that time for life on your planet it was so hot and then a massive comet that hit your planet that came from the constellation you call Capricorn. It cooled it into what you have now with your oceans and continents. It was a spectacular event when we watched it happen on our planet. When the comet hit Earth it dumped all of its waters on Earth. Then it bounced off and got caught up in

Earth's gravitational field and became your Moon. What we didn't know was that soon after that is when we were bombarded with the meteor shower that destroyed my planet. (Admiral Benson) That's an incredible story Venal. We always wanted to know how we started out in this solar system. Now thanks to you we have an eyewitness. See you already have started to help us. (Venal) Admiral there is one more thing I want to tell you since you told me about the Arcons. We were almost finished building a underground air base that was on the other side of the planet. When the meteors first started to hit our planet and they're were over 800 spacecraft there. Some fighter crafts there too, I believe. We never had to use the fighter crafts too much. But they flew them every now and then anyway. This air base was almost as deep into the surface of Mars as our laboratory. I do not know how far a long they were. But there might even be some more survivors. I do not know if they had life support chambers or not but the air craft's may be there. Who knows how many people could have gotten down there. Then the Admiral said, well I promise you this Venal if there is more of your people down there we will find your people and save all of them if it's at all possible. (Venal) Thank you Admiral you are a kind and descent people. We will never forget what you have done for us this I promise you. Then the Admiral said you're welcome, but I bet if the circumstance was reversed you would have probably have done the same thing for us. Then the Admiral gave David a communiqué and told him what was going on. Also to tell Commander Craft to move the Aurora on the other side of Mars so we can do a survey and x-ray the planet on the other side for a underground air base. Then the Admiral said to Venal, sir it has been my greatest pleasure in my entire life to be a part of helping you and your people. I thank you for coming to this meeting on such short notice. I'm going to go ahead and go back to the bridge but I really enjoyed talking to you.

If you are having any kind of problem or if you just want to talk to me about anything please don't hesitate to give me a communiqué ok? Yes Admiral Venal replied, thank you again sir. The Admiral and Venal got up and Venal went back to the hospital. The Admiral went back to the bridge to be with everyone when we go on the other side of Mars. About ten minutes later he was back at his Station on the bridge. David walked over to the Admiral to talk to him about the air base. (David) Admiral I just wanted to tell you that venal gave Dr. Kopeck the approximant location of the airbase on the electronic map and just called us and gave it to us. We really do not need to x-ray the other side unless you think there might be something else down there. Then Admiral Benson said, why don't we go head and go over there and x-ray the other side. That way we can say we done it. You know there might just be something else besides the air base over there, who knows? I know one thing there might be more people over there. We could use all of them ships too, if they're any good. One thing for sure we will find out if we go look. Then David said, very good sir. (Admiral Benson) Commander Craft lets proceed to the other side of Mars for yet one more expedition. (Commander Craft) Yes sir, Lieutenant Fisher take us to the other side of Mars on slow impulse speed please. (Lieutenant Fisher) Yes sir Commander. They started moving around slowly on impulse and before you know it they were there. Then David put in the location that Venal gave them and then they X-rayed Mars. Sure enough there was three huge Cavity's on this side, they were about 300 kilometers apart from each other. One of them was right where Venal said. (David) Sir I believe that I found the location Venal told us about and there is two other large cavities' on this side of Mars sir, besides this one. I have the one that Venal told us about locked in and it looks intact sir. I am also showing a lot of different types of metals and shapes in the cavity on sensors. (Admiral Benson) Ok Commander Braymer lets send a couple of shuttles on an expedition and just see what all is down there. Commander Braymer do you want to go on the expedition, it would be nice to have a Science Officer there? (David) I would love to sir. I will go ahead and go to the shuttle bay now. (Admiral Benson) Commander Craft just have everyone meet at shuttle bay number 10. (Commander Craft) Yes sir. David went ahead and went down to the shuttle bay and waited for everyone to get there and before you know it they were off. The shuttles started to approach a very long and rectangular hill on Mars at the location Venal gave him and landed at the supposed base in the end of the rectangle part of the hill. There was an opening into the base of the hill but there was too much sand and debris over the opening covering up what looks like might be an aircraft hanger door. They were going to have to make the opening with a devise called the ground gopher.

There were four of them, and they were totally robotic. The ground gophers were also pretty quick, and was kind of fun to watch them work. What they did was move through the dirt and rock like a bucket and scoop some up, then it would analyze it and then melt it into a liquid Then it would get another scoop, they could hold more that way. They would move it out of the way and pour it out in a pile. They were also good tunnel makers, great for laying pipe and mining.

They could tunnel straight down to strike oil or water and then blow out the top of the hole when it broke through, and still be ok and go on and do more. You could also use it under water to analyze the ocean floor for life or minerals or a camera, we mainly always used them to send on an unmanned rocket to explore and analyze a moon or and unknown planet.

You could also program them to make different shapes of very strong brick out of the liquid. The gopher can analyze the soil before it melts it and see if there are any life forms or precious stones or valuable minerals or even anything unknown to us. It would not melt it before a thorough analysis. It would even check for water or oil. It's a walking laboratory and a construction miracle and also an archaeologist and a miner.

It even checked for fossils before it starts melting everything in the bucket. It was an amazing piece of machinery for space exploration or home use. Well believe it or not it took them 45 minutes to totally clear the door way and it was 17 feet down and approximately 30 meters long. They had to cut their way through the door with a couple of lasers, you could feel and here a vacuumed sucking shush sound when they got the door opened. You could feel yourself being pulled in by the vacuum it was so strong, When everyone got inside they had to go down a walk way that was the size of the aircraft hanger door about 1000 feet down. Finally they came to another door and broke through that door and the suction was like it was when they opened the first door. When they all walked through the doorway they could see a hanger sure enough. It took their breath away when they seen all of the aircraft that was in the underground structure. They were covered with a thin coat of ice. There was water everywhere. Somehow they still looked like they were intact and in half way descent shape. They looked like they were made out of some sort of plastic compound but how could all of the electronics have lasted 120,000 years. How could these materials not have eroded or disintegrated over time. Maybe it's because the facility was buried totally air tight and it was so cold from being frozen solid all of this time in here like a freezer for 120,000 years. The hanger is air tight and the aircraft are air tight. That has to be the reason. That's incredible. We learn something everyday it seems like. (David) Ok everyone lets split up and go look for life support chambers. There might be some so keep your eyes peeled and look for hidden doors. Let's just see what's down here. This just might take some time. Everyone headed off in their own direction. The hanger was a pretty good size facility and there were rooms all around the hanger section where the aircraft were. Back on the Aurora the Admiral was receiving a communiqué from Earth and the Powleens. The Arcons and the Thracians have attacked the Powleens all over the universe in large numbers. They were now at war everywhere with the Powleens, where they had ships. There was still no sign of the Arcons or Thracians in our solar system. But that doesn't mean they aren't coming or hiding out there somewhere.

They do have cloaking devices. They weren't attacking Sybon yet either probably because the Powleens are too strong there or they're still in the planning mode. The Powleens said they have over 2000 ships. So I bet that's why the Powleens haven't been attacked on their home planet. I hope the Powleens kick their butt's before they get here. The universe would be a better place without the Arcons. In the communiqué Earth said that the Powleens were going to send some ships. But only when there is positive confirmation that the Arcons or Thracians are in Earths solar system. They are only attacking the Powleens and the Powleens do not want to drag Earth into this unless the Arcons do like last time. They could have caused a lot of damage if they hit us here by surprise. At least we have been warned, Thank God. Mean while back on Mars David and the rest of the expedition was going through every room and most of them had to be broke into. Then David received a communiqué from one of his men, Sergeant McCain and low and behold they found more life support chambers. Everyone rushed over to them and there must have been a couple of hundred more Martians and a little over 100 more different types of animals. David contacted the Aurora and told Admiral Benson and he told Venal. Venal was so excited and happy that we found more Martians, you could tell he loved us. Well the Admiral sent down 3 more shuttles and we were getting pretty good at this.

One by one we would open the life supports and we had oxygen ready and off they went, when one shuttle was full, it went to the Aurora and then it would empty out and come right back for another load. One after another for the next 10 hours until they were done. The Admiral was with Venal in the hospital helping out all that they could, so were a lot of the Martians, those that were well enough. It was a good thing that we had a full crew. Everyone was working like clockwork. All of the shuttles were starting to arrive back at the Aurora. Just about everyone headed straight for their home everyone was so beat. David arrived back to his place he came in and noticed that Heather had gone and left a note on the monitor. The note said how she really enjoyed the last two days but she didn't want to force herself on to me. David was kind of hoping Heather was here but he understood. David was also figuring that Heather would probably want to get to know her new place and I don't blame her. David went ahead and grabbed something to eat and sat down and started watching their Aurora news hour. They were calling it the daily news, but they changed it when we named the ship the Aurora. So they changed the name of the Daily news to the Aurora news hour. David went ahead and ate.

Took a shower and then went to bed for a good night sleep he was absolutely beat. He told his computer to wake him up in 6 hours and about 2 minutes later he was out like a light. The computer turned off all of the lights that were on. About 4 hours later on the bridge, (Lieutenant Courtney) Commander Craft I am picking up multiple radiation trails coming from the constellation of Gamma Hydra the Dragon sir. They are splitting up in four different directions. About a third of them are headed towards our solar system sir. (Commander Craft) Go to yellow alert Lieutenant also Contact Earth and tell them and alert the fleet. What's there ETA Lieutenant. Sir on their present course and speed they should be here in about 23 hours sir. They are coming at a high rate of speed, almost light speed sir. Sir the Kawaka is returning to Earth for its defense. Then the Lieutenant hit the yellow alert button. You could hear the navy whistle and yellow lights were flashing everywhere on the ship. David woke up and hurried to get dressed. The Admiral was already up and was on his way to the bridge. In walked the Admiral and said what do we have Commander? Sir we have multiple sightings of radiation trails all over the universe and about a third of them are headed in this direction. (Admiral Benson) Commander just how many are we talking about coming this direction? (Commander Craft) Sir theirs over 75 ships headed this way. Admiral Benson said 75 ships coming this way. That's a lot of ships Lieutenant, Contact the Powleens immediately Lieutenant and tell them what's going on. (Lieutenant Courtney) Yes sir, minutes later, Sir I contacted the Powleens and they verified what I told them and they are sending a large armada to back us as we speak. (Admiral Benson) Man I feel better knowing that. Ok people we've got to be on our toes on this one or we're in a lot of trouble, let's do it by the book. Lieutenant when the ships get close to our solar system you hit that red alert. (Lieutenant Courtney) Yes sir. About 20 minutes later, everyone is at battle station sir. (Admiral Benson) Lieutenant I want you to look around really good for possibly a couple of scout ships that might already be in our solar system hiding somewhere. (Lieutenant Courtney) Yes sir, about ten minutes went by. Sir I believe I might have something on the other side of Jupiter. There seems to be a lot of radiation emitting on the backside of Jupiter. It is an abnormally large amount of radiation sir, that normally isn't there. (Admiral Benson) Lieutenant you keep a keen eye on Jupiter. The minute you see something come out of there you go to red alert.

(Lieutenant Courtney) Yes sir! I have set our computer to watch Jupiter to sir. If there is any kind of movement the computer will go to full red alert immediately sir. Admiral the Lunar Base 3 was in route to Jupiter. It is approximately three quarters of the way there. (Admiral Benson) Lieutenant tell the Lunar Base 3 to return to Earth and set up a defensive position With Lunar Base 2, as soon as possible. (Lieutenant Courtney) Yes sir. Finally David walked into the bridge and went over and started monitoring his station. Hello Commander I'm glad you're on the bridge we could use you right now. We have just spotted a possible couple of Arcon ships on the other side of Jupiter and there are about 75 ships headed this way from the Constellation of Gamma Hydra. David raised his eye broils and gave a worried look. They are attacking the Powleens all over the place. I have just instructed the Lieutenant to go to red alert the minute something comes out from behind Jupiter. The ETA of the other Arcon ships is about 23 hours away. We told the Powleens and they are sending an armada of warships to come and help us. When David heard that last part you could tell from the look on his face that he relaxed a lot after hearing about the Powleens coming to help. (David) Wow Admiral, I only slept for about four hours. Thank God for the Powleens, They are heaven sent.

A lot sure does go on around here when you sleep. Then David kept his eye on his instruments and didn't take them off. Then he seen all of the Powleen ships and there radiation trails. They were headed this way. Sir I am showing a large armada of ships coming from the An tares region. They are going four times the speed of light sir. It looks like about fifty ships sir. They were farther away from us sir than the Arcons but the Powleens will be here one hour before they do sir. (Admiral Benson) Very good Commander. Lieutenant Courtney contact the Armory and see if that new gun is on active duty at present. (Lieutenant Courtney) I'm on it now sir, a couple of minutes later the Lieutenant said, sir the Armory has confirmed that the big gun is up an working but he advised us that we would have to rotate the ship like the old tanks use to be. Until we can line up the target. We only have a 30 degree play that we can target a ship down here because we are round, but other than that they couldn't wait to fire the Martian weapon at the Arcons. The Admiral started laughing and said I sure feel better having that Martian gun on board. David said out loud, me too sir. Plus the Admiral was also happy about putting the big guns on Earth. He knew now that it was the right thing to do. You could tell the Admiral couldn't wait to fire that weapon too. It was our ace in the hole card. He was a little worried that we hadn't test fired it yet and the fact that it's over 120,000 years old. The Admiral had a good hunch that it was going to work, somehow all of the other weapons did. Then the Admiral had Lieutenant Courtney put him on the loud speaker threw out the ship. The Admiral proceeded to tell everyone what we were all facing. Everyone felt that we had a good chance to win this because of the Powleens and all of their Warships were headed this way. We were a little outnumbered but not when you see that we have all of these Moon ships. We figured that one Moon ship is equal to two of their ships easily. Because every time they take on the Powleens they lose two or three of their ships to one of the Powleens ships. Back on Mars Captain Dopar was in charge of the second shift on the expedition. They suddenly found another big gun. They also found some more hand held weapons. They called the Aurora and told them and the Admiral asked them to get that big gun operating as soon as possible because of our new guests that are coming. Then the Admiral up dated Captain Dopar on what all was happening. Captain Dopar was turning out to be not only a loyal soldier. Also he was a blessing on anything he would help at.

The Powleens were so intelligent. The Admiral felt we were so lucky just for even knowing them. Suddenly the ship went red alert. The Admiral said that wasn't me. Then David said, no sir it was my sensors at my station. Sir the Arcons must know we are on to them they are headed for the Lunar Base three sir. Everyone it's very important to follow my orders to the letter from here on out. Lieutenant Fisher set a course to intercept the Arcons at light 4 speed. Don't worry people we have a very good chance we could win this one. (Lieutenant Fisher) Sir course plotted and our ETA is 6 minutes sir. Then the Aurora started pulling out away from Mars on one third impulse and as it reached a certain distance away from Mars it vanished into a flash of light. (Lieutenant Courtney) Admiral, There are 5 Arcon ships headed for the LB3 and the Lunar Base 3 has stopped and has split into three sections and is at Battle stations sir. (Lieutenant Fisher) Sir ETA is 3 minutes. The Arcons are real close to the LB3. They will get there before us sir. (Admiral Benson) Lieutenant Parsons prepare to fire all weapons according to which side of the ship our enemies are on except for the big gun. Lieutenant Parsons you will have to target the big gun by communiqué between you and the Armory. When we are under fire you coordinate with the Armory on targeting the Arcon ships. Lieutenant Parsons it will be up to you to say fire to the Armory. (Lieutenant Fisher) Sir ETA to the Arcons in 1-minute sir. (Admiral Benson) Ok everybody let's get ready to rumble. (Lieutenant Courtney) Sir the Arcons have engaged the LB3 and has opened fire on it sir. The LB3 has returned fire on the Arcons sir. Lieutenant Parsons start trying to get locked in for a shot at this angle and distance. Tell me when we can fire the big gun at the Arcons. Sir three of the Arcons ships has veered off of the LB3 and is heading our way sir. Sir we believe that we have a lock on one of the two ships that are attacking the LB3. (Admiral Benson) Fire that weapon Lieutenant Parsons. The Lieutenant said yes sir, and told the Armory to fire the weapon. There was no recoil, it was a yellow beam and it hit the target and 3 seconds later it exploded. Then the Admiral said I love that weapon then he said all stop and get ready to fire all weapons. Suddenly the other Arcon ship that was attacking the LB3 ceased fired and started drifting. Then the Arcon ships reached the Aurora and opened fired on the Aurora and one of them turned and went back toward the LB3 and there was only two fighting the Aurora. Then the admiral immediately said fire all weapons that you can on this side of the ship unless they move around to our backside. The Aurora opened up with all they had. Lieutenant Parsons was aligned and ready two fire the big gun. Then she said fire the big gun, suddenly it fired and 3 seconds later the ship exploded but this time it was too close and the explosion blew the Aurora back about a mile in space but their shields held up. There was some minor damage. It did the same thing to the other Arcon ship, it blew it back about a mile but they wouldn't stop firing at the Aurora. So the Admiral said do you have them lined up yet Lieutenant Parsons? (Lieutenant Parsons) Sir we have them locked in now. (Admiral Benson) Fire that weapon Lieutenant. The Lieutenant told the Armory to fire the weapon and 3 seconds later the Arcon ship exploded. Everyone cheered. Then the Admiral said lets go help the LB3 and get that other snake bastard. They weren't far from the LB3 and they were going at it with the last Arcon ship. One of the sections of the LB 3 has taken a lot of hits and is in a lot of trouble at the moment but they just kept firing all of their weapons. Then suddenly it exploded and all were lost on the base section of the LB3. The other two sections just kept on firing at the Arcon ship with all of their weapons. Then one of the last two sections were starting to drift but it would not stop firing their weapons. As the Aurora was rushing towards the LB3 the Admiral said Lieutenant Parsons do you have a lock on this last Arcon ship? I do now sir. Fire that weapon Lieutenant. Then the Lieutenant told the Armory to fire and they fired but they were still a little off their target but when it finally started hitting the target suddenly after about 12 seconds the last Arcon ship exploded. It was close to the LB3 and it knocked back both of the sections that were left but it looked like their shields held up. Then Lieutenant Courtney called the LB3 and you could hear the Lieutenant say LB3 this is the Aurora are you ok? Then Admiral Feeney answered and said, yes what's left of us is just fine now. Then everyone cheered again and the Admiral said lets go give them some help. (Commander Braymer) Admiral the Powleens ETA is 5 hours away and the Arcons are about 5 and a half hours away sir. (Admiral Benson) Lieutenant Courtney I need a damage report on the Aurora and the LB3. (Lieutenant Courtney) Yes sir, a few minutes later Admiral I have the casualty report from the LB3 sir. They lost 542 people and some 200 injuries. One of their sections have been totally destroyed and one of the last two sections have engine damage but the other section is ok sir.

The Aurora had no injuries just little minor damage on the outside of the ship. But there was no hull breach and shields were fine. (Admiral Benson) Lieutenant Courtney contact Admiral Feeney and see if they can still connect the last two sections of their ship together. We will put our tractor beam on them and then we will take them back to Mars with us for repairs. It doesn't matter if they cannot connect them. We can still put both of their ship sections on the tractor beam and take them to Mars with us. (Lieutenant Courtney) Yes sir. Sir they are trying to connect now. Then the Aurora decloaked out of light speed and then came in on half impulse. They came close to the LB3 on quarter impulse. Finally stopped in front of the LB3. (Lieutenant Courtney) The LB3 sir has affirmed connection to its other section. Open up a communiqué with Admiral Feeney on the LB3 and myself, Lieutenant. Hello Admiral Feeney how is the rest of your crew? Hello Admiral Benson thanks to you and that new weapon of yours you save our necks. I wish we had one of those Martian weapons. We probably wouldn't have lost a third of my crew. I know Admiral Feeney I'm sorry we couldn't have got to you sooner. We got here as quick as we could. I know you did Admiral. I lost my second in command and a lot of decent people but they didn't die in vain. The crew of the LB3 was really sad and some of them were crying because they had lost a lot of their crew most of them friends and family.

Admiral Feeney the crew of the Aurora and myself are so sorry for your lose, we fill your sorrow, they died very bravely. I will note that in my Captains log and all of you are going to get promoted. I know that doesn't make up for all of your loses but all of us feel your lose and you have our condolences Admiral. (Admiral Feeney) Thank you Admiral for saving us. Then Admiral Benson said anytime you need help my friend you just say the word. Now we do not have much time so I will now lock on to your ship with our tractor beam and take you back with us to Mars for repairs. (Admiral Feeney) Thanks again for everything Admiral. Then the Aurora's tractor beam grabbed the LB3 and they were headed back to Mars.

Admiral Benson you have a communiqué from the President, I am patching you through on COM sir. Hello Mr. President how did you like the battle sir? Hello Admiral Benson, That was a great victory Admiral we were all cheering on Earth for you and the LB3. You don't know it yet but your famous on Earth, I also want to thank everyone and to give my condolences to all of the people that were lost.

It was a costly battle, but all of the men and women on board the LB3 and the Aurora are heroes on Earth and the people that gave their lives will not be forgotten. I promises you this Admiral. They all died for the People on Earth and Mars. I'm going to call and tell the LB3 the same thing after I talk to you. We will never forget your sacrifice. I also know that there is another battle that we are about to face. Our hopes and prayers are with all of you and always remember this we may be down on Earth but our hearts and souls and Earth's future is with all of you out there in space. Remember this that if you lose your lives fighting our enemy's, you will never be forgotten. This I promise you. That Marian weapon was god sent wasn't it Admiral.

I'm sure glad we have two of them on Earth thanks to you Admiral and your Science Officer Commander Braymer. (Admiral Benson) We are just doing our jobs sir. We also thank everyone on Earth for his or her prayers and support. Now sir I guess we are at war with a race of people in another galaxy we don't even know.

Sir I'm just going to go back to Mars and set up a defensive posture between Earth and Mars. Because we have two big gun weapons on Mars and we have one on our ship. We could do a lot of damage to our enemy before they can get to you. But Mr. President if they out flank us we will rush to Earth and defend you to the death sir. (The President) Thanks again Admiral we will be rooting for you down here. So good luck and God speed Admiral and the gallant crew of the Aurora. (Lieutenant Courtney) Transmission ended sir. (David) Sir the Powleen fleet will be here in one and a half hour.

Sir the Arcon armada is right behind them at 2 hours away sir. (Lieutenant Fisher) Sir our ETA to Mars is 3 minutes sir. (Admiral Benson) Lieutenant Fisher lets orbit on this side of Mars but let's put the LB3 on the other side of Mars first with the LB1. They have a big gun on that side of the planet and we have a big gun on our side. When they separate there will be 5 ships that are armed with lasers and rockets over there on their side of Mars with one big gun. Us over here with two big guns one on Mars and one on the Aurora. They have to go through us to get to Earth and we are pretty well equipped. Earth has the four Powleen ships and two of the Martians big guns on Earth. Also LB2 that splits into three ships with lasers and rockets. Everyone everywhere did everything they could to prepare for a major battle. Suddenly flash after flash was appearing. There they were, all over the place. Twenty moon ships surrounded Earth.

The Whole Earth cheered the Powleens on. I really do think that at that moment in time everyone would have voted any Powleen as the next President if they were running. There were Powleen ships all over the solar system. They just kept coming Flash after flash, there were more than 50 ships. There was an excess of 500 Powleen ships all over our solar system. There was 50 radiation trails but in groups of 10. The Powleens had tricked the Arcons. Then suddenly the Arcons started to arrive. They had no Idea there were so many Powleen ships until the last minute after they arrived. They immediately went under a massive attack. There were ships crashing everywhere on all of our Planets and all of their moons in the solar system. They were becoming grave sites for all sorts of Arcon ships. It was the ultimate of all battles won. That's when they realized that afterwards they would have to go everywhere to find survivors and prisoners. They didn't know where they were going to put the prisoners. They knew that Earth would probably want them on Mars. The Admiral did not want to ruin Mars with the likes of them. Then David noticed that the Arcons sent another very large armada behind the first 75. There were so many trails coming this way from Gamma Hydra the Dragon, ETA 12 hours away. (David) Admiral I'm showing masses of ships coming this way from the constellation of Gamma Hydra the Dragon sir, there are more than I can count Admiral. The Computer estimates 642 ships sir. Don't worry Commander we will be waiting for them. This time they were spreading out trying to out flank the whole solar system. They were going to surround us and come at us at all directions. We were starting to worry a little bit but we were motivated we could see victory. This was our second victory with the Arcons. The last of the first armada of Arcons were being wiped out the minute they would uncloak. They didn't see the Powleens because they were at all stop and cloaked all over the solar system. The Powleens would start hammering the Arcons ships with all that they had one after another it was a historic battle that would decide the fate and control of the universe. We have had very few casualties so far on our side. We were so lucky the Powleens came. David counted over 6 hundred and 42 more ships coming by way of the Arcons. They were almost here. We were surrounded all over the solar system. It's like they were waiting for all of their ships to arrive and then they would come at us all at once. The Earth looked like it just gave birth to a lot of Moons. Finally they were all ready to attack. Then they came at us from all sides.

The count of ships was about equal. They had a few ships that were bigger than the others ships. It was firing a different kind of weapon than the other Arcon ships. It seemed to have more Power than the other ships. The Powleens were starting to take on a lot of damage. They had lost 20 Moon ships and it was starting to really heat up. Then everyone realized that they were Thracian ships, and they were starting to reach Mars. A horde of ships got through the backside of our solar system and opened up on everyone. There were about 30 Arcon and Thracian ships and more coming our way. The Aurora was starting to take on some damage and had lost some of their shields but they just kept on firing everything they had, you could see Mars shooting its big guns at the Enemy ships. The big land based weapons on Mars could use a form of semi automatic fire with a 2 second delay before refiring. The Aurora couldn't because of the way they had to mount it on the ship. The Arcon ships were exploding one after another from the land base gun. They were crashing all over Mars.

The LB1 and the LB3 each lost another section each, the LB3 only had one section left and there were over 1000 people dead. The Thracians were also starting to attack the surface of Mars it wasn't looking good for the Aurora either. Because we were taking on too many casualties and too much damage. The Aurora was taking too many hits but so far most of the important shields were holding. The Arcons and the Thracians first went toward the Moon Ships around Mars first before anywhere else. That's why the Aurora was taking on so much damage. The enemy sure didn't like them land base weapons. Everyone just kept firing all weapons and attacking. Eventually the two big land base weapons were doing most of the damage to the enemy ships it was an amazing thing to see. It was so accurate, one after another the alien ships just kept exploding in space over Mars. Crashing down on the planet, it had perfect accuracy. There was another group of twenty coming to Mars it was not looking good anymore. They had one of the big Thracian ships with this bunch and they were there before we could do anything. Then a group of eight Powleen moon ships and one Kawaka ship came and backed up Mars and the Aurora. If they hadn't we would have been wiped out. We just kept firing the big guns. We knew we wouldn't have had a chance without the big guns. Then the Aurora targeted the large Thracian ship and fired the big gun we had. Three seconds later the large Thracian ship exploded in a thousand pieces.

Their shields seemed useless against the Martian weapon. That's when we started to see things turning in our favor, victory was in sight. The Aurora was still taking too many hits from all of the enemy ships. Then there was an explosion and a hull breach the size of a small building. It was the North West section of the ship. Decks one through four were totally destroyed.

The Aurora lost a lot of people on that last hit. Then David realized that was Heathers place. I hope she wasn't there. Maybe she was still at the hospital helping out. What the Admiral was doing every time we would lose part of our shields or have a lot of damage the Admiral would rotate the Aurora. You could still have shields by turning the ship until it hides the bad section of the ship. On the backside away from the attacking enemy ships. David was getting more worried by the minute and then he contacted the hospital to see if Heather was still there. But it was so chaotic no one could find her but that doesn't mean that she wasn't up there somewhere.

So David said if someone finds her to have her call me. They said ok and David went back to work. The Powleens ships that came to help were all good Captains they were kicking some ass but they did lose a couple more ships. What was odd about the Arcons and the Thracians was we were stomping the hell out of their entire fleet. They must have had one mean ruler because they just wouldn't stop. David couldn't stop worrying about Heather. I hope she's all right. The enemy was starting to hurt us pretty bad. They were relentless in there attacking, there was so many of them. There were also a lot of crashed Arcon and Thracian ships on Mars. All of the people that were in them ships that survived the crash were setting up an offensive on foot against the Mars base and the big guns. Captain Dopar who was in charge of the last big gun on Mars that was found where the hanger was. Captain Dopar and a couple of his men were starting to look at some of the fighter aircraft in the underground air base. Well that Captain Dopar was pretty crafty. He was able to get a couple of the fighters figured out. Him and two other Powleens decided to try and stop all of the enemy that crashed landed on Mars. By defending the Mars base and the big guns with the Martian aircraft. There were a couple of thousand Arcons and Thracians on the ground assaults. The Martian aircraft was way ahead of even the Powleens technology. Their weapons were unstoppable. After the Powleens figured out how the aircraft worked they realized how easy they were.

They were so easy to fly a child could fly them once you knew how. Captain Dopar was very affective on the ground defending everyone with the three Martian ships. There shields were superior to anything we had. The enemy hand held lasers were like toys to the Martian ships shields on the aircraft. They could also hover too. Captain Dopar and his two buddy's would just pull right over the Arcons hovering with their shields on and open firing on the Arcons. The Arcons and the Thracians didn't have a chance against the Martian aircraft and they finally surrendered. We were really starting to outnumber them in space too. There were wrecked ships everywhere. Some of them were starting to get through to the Powleens. There were so many and they were striking some of the big cities on Earth. They were hurting a lot of people but usually they got destroyed soon afterwards. The two big guns that the Admiral put on Earth were also semi automatic fire and there were downed ships all over Earth. The Aurora seen about twenty more ships headed their way. David couldn't stop worrying about Heather so he called one more time. At first when they looked around they couldn't find Heather. But all of a sudden she walked up to Dr. Moon and the nurse seen her and told David here she is, she's right here, David would you like to talk to her? (David) I sure would, can you put her on. (Heather) Hey honey is everything ok? Did you hear about our homes? Then David started to smile and said I was worried about you. I thought you might have been at home when it happened. I am so glad you're ok Heather. Then it just popped out I love you Heather. Then Heather said I love you to David. (David) Ok honey, I will call you back in a little while to check on you. Boy I'm sure glad you weren't home Heather, bye bye. Then suddenly the Arcons and the Thracians were starting to leave Earth. We didn't know it at the time but they were on their way back home retreating. They were going to hit us on the way back. The Powleens were starting to get more of the advantage and had a lot of them on the run. But they were still doing a lot of damage and killing a lot of people. The new rush of Arcons and Thracians were starting to arrive. They just started hammering the Aurora. All of our big guns just kept blowing the enemy ships away. So was all of the Powleen ships and when the Aurora thought it was about be destroyed. They stopped to everyone's amazement pulled off and high tailed it back toward their home planet with all their other ships. Which were only about 100 of them left.

We didn't know it at the time but the Powleens had just launched an invading armada toward the Gamma Hydra constellation. To attack there two worlds and as soon as the Arcons found out what the Powleens were doing all of their ships stopped fighting us and retreated back to defend their worlds. The Powleens veered off of the Arcons world. Right before the Arcons and the Thracians got back. They did not want any more of the Powleens or of us. They did not pursue the Powleens when they veered off. They almost lost their entire space fleet. Everyone everywhere was cheering and celebrating, "We won the battle of all battles", the war that freed the Galaxy. Then suddenly Heather came to the bridge and embraced David and they kissed each other and cheered with the rest of the crew on the Aurora. Even on Sybon there was celebration and feasting all over their planet. We made it a holiday on Mars and Earth and Sybon. We had the firework celebration of all fire work shows. Everyone rounded up all of the Arcons and Thracians that had crashed on Earth and Mars and all of the other planets and Moons. All of the fighting had stopped. It was a new time to colonize Mars and a time of peace and harmony in the galaxy. Earth and the Powleens started to move to Mars to live with the Martians. They all were very happy living with each other. Who knows how long before we see the Arcons and the Thracians again. One thing for sure, it's not going to be any time soon, we hurt them to bad. The Martians were just happy to be alive again and we had a whole new outlook, a whole galaxy to explore. Now we have light speed. Stay tuned for more adventures of 1st Science Officer Commander David Braymer.

The End

38805627R00057

Made in the USA
Middletown, DE
11 March 2019